Trashland A Go-Go

THE NEW BIZARRO AUTHOR SERIES

PRESENTS

Trashland A Go-Go

CONSTANCE ANN FITZGERALD

Eraserhead Press
Portland, OR

ERASERHEAD PRESS
205 NE BRYANT
PORTLAND, OR 97211

WWW.ERASERHEADPRESS.COM

ISBN: 1-62105-002-5

Editor's Note:

Constance Ann Fitzgerald is one of my favorite people.

When I learned that she wrote vignettes about the creeps that come into the sex shop where she works, I had to read them. When I did, I asked Ms. Fitzgerald if she'd ever thought about writing bizarro fiction. She said it might be fun.

Constance Ann came to BizarroCon 2010, to see what this whole scene is about. She easily made friends and won everyone over with her idea to write a Trashy Fairy Tale about a dead stripper. So charming!

I'm very happy to be working with my friend and presenting her work to all of you. I know you'll love this delightful Mad Hatter trip into the horribly fun trashscape that Constance Ann has created. Enjoy yourselves.

I'm happy to present Constance Ann Fitzgerald's book to you as part of the New Bizarro Author Series. This is this author's first book! The NBAS strives to bring new voices in bizarro fiction to our readers. It serves as an opportunity to introduce you to new writers, and to introduce them into the world of being an author. Eraserhead Press is happy to bring new, weird voices to you in the hopes that these authors will prove themselves to be strong members of the bizarro community and continue to entertain you for years to come. The publishing of this book marks the beginning of a one year proving period. Please help support our NBAS writers in their endeavors by telling your friends about their cool new books. This book you hold is only one of several hundred that must be sold in order for this author to continue on her path. We hope you help her along as best as you can. Thank you.

~~Kevin Shamel

Author's Note:

For Andrew Wilson

Special thanks to Kevin Shamel, Kevin Parks, Brooke Morrison and the Bizarro Community

One

Coco took a deep breath, leaned back to fluff her mane of Aquanetted curls, and made sure there wasn't any blood leaking out of her nostrils. She winked at her reflection in the mirror and adjusted her hair.

Somewhere between the adrenaline rush before she hit the stage—where she felt the most adored—and the cocaine in her dressing room, she was feeling pretty fucking amazing. She rode that buzzing wave out onto the stage as the DJ boomed, "For all of you just arriving, welcome to Snatch Hausen! Where there is more than one use for a brautwurst! Talk about a happy hour special!" Coco hated it when Victor, the club's DJ, talked over the intro to her song. She would be sure to give him a good tongue-lashing after her performance.

"Gentleman, welcome Snatch Hausen's own Coco Darling!"

Coco sauntered onto the stage. Chastity brushed passed her, smirking. Normally Chastity would make some kind of catty comment in passing, or glare at her and hiss "bitch" as she stepped offstage, always too late for Coco to retaliate; the spotlight already setting her thick coat of body glitter off like twinkling oversexed stars. This time, Chastity just smirked and quietly snickered to herself as she passed. Although Coco found this strange, she strutted on, thinking that perhaps Chastity had chosen another girl as the object of her unfounded hatred.

Coco's mind cleared of all these things as the spotlight bathed and blinded her. She rolled her hips at the few men she could make out in the front row. She ran her hands up and over her silver bikini and pulled at the strings slowly, making the rounded man, whose shining crown of his head was visible through a sad comb-over, sweat and salivate. His tongue lulled slightly out the corner of his thin-lipped mouth. It was a good reaction—one that would get at least a couple of dollar bills tucked into her g-string. So she focused on him. She kept her eyes fixed on him as she approached the pole at center stage.

Coco built up a little momentum to give herself a nice solid start on the spin. But when her hands grasped the polished chrome, they held only for a brief moment before something slick and slimy caused her to lose her grip. Coco flew across the room like a semi-nude astronaut, and crashed into the DJ booth. The heel of her stiletto gouged a hole into the soundboard and sent up orange and bright violet-blue flashing sparks that snapped, popped, and finally sizzled. Plumes of smoke poured from the smoldering mess of Coco's hair.

Victor ducked behind his chair as the half-naked, airborne woman sped toward him. At slow speed, this would have been some odd sexual fantasy fulfilled for him, but Coco's speedy flight made him realize that this was not going to end even remotely like so many previous dreams about her.

"Coco...? Coco?" he called to her as he stood. "Coco?!" Victor raised his voice, shouting over the commotion of the gathering crowd.

In response, Coco slid off the soundboard and landed in front of the console with a thick, meaty thud.

Two

"Oh, she'll be just fine. She's pretty out of it. We'll go get her checked out. Lots of rest. You know the drill. She'll be back in no time!" Arnie, the club's owner, shouted after the stragglers.

Drunken men, disoriented by Coco's accident, shuffled out the door as Arnie held it for them.

Victor squatted down beside Coco, having a conversation with her. He pretended that she was responding. He pretended she had come back around. At least she had stopped smoking. The smell was overwhelming so close to her body. Burnt hair, smoked meat, and just a hint of cotton candy hung heavy in the air. The smoke blended with the fog machine and made ghostly, foul-scented shapes that faded almost as quickly as they appeared. Strobing lights of various colors pulsated through the haze.

"No, don't try and get up," Arnie said boisterously over his shoulder as he ushered the last of the customers outside.

The stone-still, topless Coco lay flat on her back in front of the DJ booth.

Victor's eyes glazed in awe as he stared down at Coco Darling.

Arnie shut and locked the door with an easy affable grin until the bolt and reinforcement bar were firmly in place. He then turned and bounded across the room to where Victor gazed at Coco.

Arnie's sudden presence was enough to snap Victor out of his daze. He shifted his eyes away from the charred, crumpled beauty with great effort and redirected his focus to his boss, who was covering his nose with the collar of his

11

shirt. Even through the fabric Arnie's expression of disgust was visible.

"What do we do now, Arnie?" Victor asked. His eyes were wide. He sounded like a frightened child.

Arnie, unaffected by the events, let the collar of his shirt fall from his bulbous nose to speak. "Seriously, Vic? What the fuck do you think? Stuff and mount her? Put her at the front door? Turn her into a coat rack? You wanna keep her a while?" Victor stared at his shoes while Arnie continued, "She already fucking reeks. Jesus, she reeks. We chuck her in the garbage." He slapped the back of Victor's head with the flat of his palm. "We wrap her in trash bags and bury her in the dumpster. Pick up should be first thing tomorrow morning. Once she's at the dump there's no telling where she came from. Strippers and hookers go missing all the fucking time, ya know? What's one more?" Arnie wiped his oily forehead with the back of his hand, and brushed sweat onto his slacks. He went to the janitor's closet.

"Really, Arnie? We're just going to dump her in the trash?" Victor asked, cocking his head to the side like a confused puppy. He stared down at Coco. If he squinted, the matted mess of hair wasn't so bad. If he breathed through his mouth he didn't smell the burned skin and layers of melted glitter. But when he exhaled, the faint taste of barbeque lingered on his tongue.

Coco had always been high strung, and more than a little mouthy, but in her voltage-induced slumber she seemed so peaceful. Lying there she looked like a sleeping Amazon from outer space; a topless alien race napping at Victor's feet. He thought she must look lovelier than she ever had before, and what a shame it was. The only time she shut her mouth long enough for Victor to truly appreciate her unique beauty up close, not just in his head, and she had to go and be dead the whole time.

Arnie thrust a roll of trash bags into Victor's hands. "Stop gaping at this bitch and get busy wrapping. Start at her head. I'll start at her feet." Arnie licked his lips thinking about Coco's feet.

During Snatch Hansen's *More Than One Use for a Brautwurst Happy Hour*, customers chose strippers for private dances and paid extra for them to act out sexual fantasies with the sausages. Arnie often chose Coco to lick the brauts and run her dainty, manicured digits over the casings before smooshing them between her toes. He never paid her, but he owned the club and felt he deserved the perks. Who would argue with him? All of the girls knew just how replaceable they were.

Arnie started wrapping Coco's feet in black plastic. He took his time until he reached her ankles. Then his interest waned and he went about his work quickly.

"C'mon Vic, she ain't getting any fresher."

Victor held Coco's head in the open palm of his hand. The trash bag only covered her forehead. He stared at her closed eyelids and searched for a final sign of life. He hoped she would cough and twitch back into existence, but he couldn't cradle her corpse all night—as strong as the urge might be. Arnie was growing impatient. "What the fuck, Victor? What's the fucking hold-up?"

Victor shook the warm thoughts of cold parts away and wrapped the rest of her head quickly while looking up at Arnie. He didn't want to see Coco's pallid face, smudged with grey, swallowed up by the black plastic.

"No hold-up, man." Victor stammered. "It's just weird. I mean, what are the chances…"

"Do you really fucking care? We need to get her outta here before the night cleaning crew shows up." Arnie snapped.

They wrapped her from head to toe in layers of thirty-three gallon heavy duty trash bags and finished it all off with a somewhat festive looking knot cinched at her waist.

"Let's go chuck her in the dumpster and get a drink," Arnie said. He picked Coco up by her ankles and dragged her several feet. "I ain't doing this by myself, man. Grab a handful of head there and let's get movin'."

Victor squatted low, cupped his hands around the back of her head, cradling it delicately, and lifted from his knees. They grunted and heaved as they carried her out the side

13

entrance and into the alley. When they reached the dumpster, they each fumbled with the palm-sweated plastic to readjust their grip.

"How'd she fly off like that anyways?" Victor wondered aloud.

"That little bitch, Chastity. She went on right before this one here." He swung Coco by the legs. "They've been at each other's throats since she started here. I think Chastity wiped some Vaseline or something on the pole before she got off the stage. Sneaky bitch. We'll deal with her tomorrow. Right now we just need to dump this one."

They counted to three and swung Coco back and forth, creating enough momentum (the same force that caused her demise) to fling her into the dumpster. At *three*, they both let go and launched their black plastic bandaged mummy into the pile of trash. Glass clinked against glass, tin and aluminum cans crunched, and papers rustled.

Coco sank into the quicksand refuse.

Arnie grabbed a few flattened cardboard boxes and tossed them over her in an attempt to hide the human-shaped garbage pile. He slapped Victor's back and slung an arm around his shoulder. "Now, I don't know about you, but I need a fucking drink!"

Victor nodded and looked over his shoulder as he walked down the alley. He was surprised at how hidden Coco already was.

She was magic.

Three

Coco woke feeling incredibly warm and a little sweaty.

When she tried to touch her face, she found she could not move her arms at all. She opened her eyes, and more blackness greeted her, the sight of which set panic aflame.

Coco began to breathe heavily and her mouth filled with the slick texture and flavor of plastic. She exhaled. The heat and condensation from her breath lingered around her face. She concentrated on moving her arm, and managed to stretch the cocoon and wriggle her hand free. Coco immediately poked a hole through the plastic over her mouth with a long, polished, acrylic fingernail. She took a deep breath while she stripped off her wrapping.

The stench of hot garbage blasted Coco. She freed her right hand, and with both hands she managed to tear away the layers covering her face and neck. She sat up, feet and legs still bound, and glared out into the bright sunlight.

"The fucking dump?!" she shouted to no one.

Looking around, only able to see as far as her head could turn, Coco was shocked to find herself laying on a bed of discarded potato chip bags, egg shells, cheeseburger wrappers, soda and beer bottles, and who-knew-what-else beneath. It all smelled terrible. And something smelled vaguely singed.

Singed. Burned. Electrified.

It all came back to her; the slickness of the chrome, Chastity's obnoxious smirk as she exited the stage, and flying into the DJ booth.

"That miserable whore!" shouted Coco with enough force that she toppled over and rolled down the small garbage hill. She sat up and unwound the plastic binding around her feet, knees and thighs, only to realize that underneath the layers of trash bags she wore only her silver g-string. That was when it dawned on her: "Those bastards. They just… threw me away?"

Coco stood and assessed her situation. No matter which direction she looked, all she could see was more trash—an outwardly endless expanse of waste all around her. Flies gathered and landed before departing again. They hopped from one pile of trash to another. The buzzing in the air sounded like faint whispers.

There was no way she could clamber through the landfill in her stilettos. She looked down at them and realized that the buckle of one was burned into the flesh of her ankle. She screamed and swore as she yanked the embedded metal from her skin.

She tore squares of cardboard from a nearby box and wrapped her feet with the strips of the leftover plastic that she had torn away from her legs. Coco looked down at her handiwork and decided that although not as fashionable as her heels, they would be much more functional. Nothing about her current ensemble was fashionable. It was made entirely of trash bags.

After peeling away the layers of plastic from her face and legs, what remained was a strapless number, knotted in the middle, and ending above her knees, paired with plastic-wrapped cardboard-soled shoes.

Coco sighed deeply, "Well, I guess there's no one out here to impress, anyway."

She picked a direction, figuring that no matter where she walked, she'd eventually come to the end of the landfill. From there she could convince some stupid man to drive her home where she would press charges against Arnie and Chastity.

Assholes.

Four

Coco was getting tired. Despite the smell of ripeness all around her, she was hungry too. There were miles of food around her, but all of it was beyond spoiled. It seemed to mock her with its presence and inedibility.

She found a relatively smooth surface on one of many hills made of trash, where she could sit and rest. She picked through the pile for small items and tossed them at a nearby row of aluminum cans, knocking them down. Coco was surprised by her good aim. She enjoyed the sound of the items as they hit the cans. A bottle cap: *Tink!* An apple core: *Thump!* An old magic marker: *Plunk!*

Coco continued to search for things to throw, pleased that she had found a way to amuse herself. She dug around a bit more, unable to find anything else small enough to toss at the cans. She gave up her game and decided to kick the cans down for closure.

A small black fly zipped out from the mouth of a large can of beer marketed as being Australian, but that was really just disgusting. Out of contempt for that vile tasting beer, Coco smashed the can beneath her cardboard-clad foot and found a mild satisfaction in the sound of something being crushed and broken.

Five

"What the fuck?!" shouted a small, furious voice.

Coco spun in a slow circle, looking for the owner of the voice. There was no one to be seen.

A small black fly landed on the tip of Coco's nose.

As she went to swat it away she heard the voice again. "That was my fucking house! What the fuck is wrong with you?! Where am I going to live?!"

Coco stared cross-eyed at the fly for a moment in disbelief as it vomited orange liquid all over the tip of her nose.

"Gross!" She squealed and swatted at the insect.

"Gross?!" the fly shouted, buzzing around her head. "I'll tell you what's gross! An inconsiderate bitch running around tormenting folks and squashing their homes with her giant barbarian feet!"

Coco was stunned. "My feet are *not* that... This fly *isn't* really talking to me." She shook her head vigorously, trying to empty it of the delusions of talking flies.

"The hell I'm not!" the fly spat angrily. He buzzed back and forth from the trampled can and orbited Coco's head. "What a day! What a fucking day!" said the fly, obviously distressed. "First I find out that I only have a week to live. A *week*! Can you imagine?" he said, buzzing so close to Coco's face that she found herself cross-eyed again trying to focus on him.

"That's terrible," Coco said. She suddenly felt bad for having crushed that can.

"And *now*," the fly ranted, "now I've nowhere to live for that week! What am I going to do?"

The fly landed, and collapsed into the folds of a rotting

orange. He began to cry squeaky little sobs, which were probably considered quite large for a creature its size.

Coco sat on a pile of Styrofoam containers beside the rotting orange and its sobbing, sniffling resident. "It can't be too terribly hard for a *fly* to find a place to live in a *dump*? But I'm sorry."

She picked up the crinkled can and peered into its mouth. Sure enough there was a mini smashed sofa, a television with a shattered screen and snapped-off antennas and a crumpled end table complete with a destroyed reading lamp and tiny tattered magazines. Some of which were pornographic.

Coco put the can down, blinked feverishly, and shook her head some more. She grabbed the can again and peered back inside. All of its contents were still there, but shaken up to resemble the bits in a kaleidoscope. She turned the can upside down, convinced that what she was seeing was an optical illusion. As an erotic dancer, she knew all about smoke and mirrors—lighting was key. The bits of furniture and miniature magazines rattled. Several articles tumbled out and fell into the trash at Coco's feet.

The fly, nestled in the decaying fruit, had just started to calm down and breathe evenly. He looked up with sixteen teary lenses in time to see his crushed possessions poured out of his home like the god-awful swill it once held. He dropped his tiny, fuzzy face back into the orange, and began to sob again.

Coco sat atop the pile of to-go containers and put the can down carefully. Sticky bits of mashed French fries coated in thick, congealed remnants of ketchup and mustard stuck to her calves. She flicked it off quickly with her long, dirty acrylic nails. She couldn't believe what was happening. She thought she must be unconscious.

Perhaps it was just that wavy-looking dream sequence like in the movies. The part where she would eventually awake in a hospital bed must be next. But upon thinking all of these things, Coco realized that she still wasn't waking up. The fly was bawling his tiny, multi-lensed eyes out into a piece of rotting fruit. The smell of the dump was still absolutely vile and Coco was STILL hungry.

Six

Victor finished his drink and reached for his wallet.

Arnie cocked an eyebrow at him and took a long slow swallow from his glass. He set it down on the battered bar and the ice clinked inside the empty tumbler. "You want another?" he asked Victor.

"No, thanks. I think I'll go home. Get some rest." Victor really wanted another drink. He wanted ten. But he couldn't stand to look at Arnie's pock-marked sleazy face any longer.

They were a few blocks from Snatch Hausen, at another bar—a dank sort of hole-in-the-wall, with a jukebox that still played the same records it had for the last thirty years. The records were warped and scratched. The music came out warbly and skipped often. None of the bar's few patrons seemed to mind, or even seemed to be listening. It served as more of a melodic white noise. Something to keep the quiet out while they sat at the bar on cracked leather barstools, patched with duct and electrical tape, drowning their troubles.

Victor took some cash from his wallet and Arnie shook his head. "Naw man, I got this one. I'll see you tomorrow at six, yeah?" Arnie slapped Victor's back for the millionth time that night.

It was Arnie's own brand of comradery that Victor was growing to hate. Almost as much as he had grown to hate Arnie himself in the few hours they sat drinking together.

Victor put the money back in his wallet. He couldn't turn down a free drink. "Yeah, Arnie. Six o'clock."

Arnie stood up, leaning heavily onto the bar to steady himself. He was drunk and looked at Victor through one squinted eye. "See ya' then. I'm going to hit the head." He hiccupped and pounded his fist on the bar before walking away.

Arnie staggered to the back of the bar. He weaved between the tables and chairs with swaying steps as though caught in a howling wind. Victor sighed and rose from his stool. He eyed the off-sale liquor for only a split second before deciding to get a bottle of whiskey for the road.

Victor walked back toward Snatch Hausen with heavy, sluggish feet. He was far too drunk to drive home and he lived too far away to walk. He didn't feel much like wasting money on cab fare, so he opted to sleep in his car in the parking lot of the club and drive home in the morning.

He chugged from the bottle as he walked down the street. He didn't care if the police stopped him. He almost hoped they would. He felt guilty about Coco. Throwing her in the garbage was obviously not the right thing to do. Anyone with a general sense of right and wrong knew that. But panic had taken over, guided by intimidation. He had seen what happened to people who crossed Arnie. He wasn't someone you wanted to fuck with.

Victor's thought process was impeded by the now half-empty bottle of cheap whiskey. He took his usual shortcut down the alley that spilled out into the deserted parking lot of Snatch Hausen. It wasn't until the dumpster was only a few feet from him that he realized what a terrible idea the shortcut had been. Victor stared at the dumpster and his eyes welled with hot, salty tears. He never got to tell her how he felt about her.

He was disgusted with his own cowardice. He worked with Coco for three months and somehow had never found the courage to ask her out, or even hold any kind of conversation with her. He leaned against the side of the dumpster. The metal was cold against his back as he gradually slid down onto the asphalt and began to weep.

Victor sat there for some time with the open bottle of whiskey in his lap, sobbing in front of the dumpster where he and Arnie had disposed of the late great Coco Darling. His darling Coco. If only he could tell her how he felt. If only he could have stood up to Arnie. Oh, if only.

Victor stood up, stumbling over his feet and wiped his eyes with the sleeve of his shirt before wiping his nose with the other—leaving two moist streaks behind each nostril. He sniffed and stared at the dumpster.

The squashed cardboard boxes were still as Arnie had left them. Somewhere in there was Coco, as lovely as ever. Only in need of a sponge bath. At the very least, he thought he could tell her how he felt.

He thought he could stand in the alleyway and spill his guts about the hours he spent admiring her. How lovely he thought she was. How badly he needed to be near her, and feel her supple skin pressed against his tense body. The idea of saying these things to a mound of trash did not appeal to him. Nor did the possibility of someone wandering by and listening to him wail his professions of love into the night. But he couldn't shake his yearning—the all-consuming need to be near her. So he did the most reasonable thing he could think to do.

Victor pulled himself up the side of the dumpster and swung his leg over the ledge. He sat straddling the dumpster's edge and looked around to make sure there was no one else to witness him diving into the trash receptacle. Once he saw that the coast was clear, Victor swung his other leg over and fell haplessly into the dumpster. He lay there for a moment in the trash heap.

"Ssshhtupid fuckin' whissshkey," he slurred.

The dumpster began to spin around him. He groaned and rolled onto his belly. He lay atop a piece of cardboard, reached below it with one hand and dug around in the garbage for something that resembled Coco.

He felt the smooth surface of many plastic bags as he groped blindly for the one unyielding bag that contained his departed love. His hand wrapped around something more solid. Something long and slender that did not give way to his firm grip. Victor's breath quickened as he poked holes through the plastic with clumsy, drunken fingers, to tear open the plastic casing and caress his beloved Coco. He told himself it wasn't sick. That he wasn't doing anything wrong, no matter how aroused he was getting at the thought of her waiting beneath that plastic for his touch. Just for him.

Something smelled awful. This did not come as a complete surprise to Victor as he was well aware that he was inside a dumpster, but he refused to let the slightly woozy feeling creeping into his stomach diminish the gratification he knew he would surely feel. He told himself it was closure. That he was just saying goodbye the best way he knew how.

The layers of plastic were slick with fluids from the dumpster and his hands slipped as he tore through the bag. The anticipation was killing him. He let his hand drift up the length of the bag, feeling what seemed to be her thigh. He pictured her legs as they had been on stage—taunting him under red lights, wrapped around the chrome pole, grinding on the stage. He slipped a finger into the bag and felt the sponginess of flesh.

Victor was so overcome that he began to pant like a dog as he tore through the remaining plastic separating him from his love. When the contents were finally free, underneath the dim orange glow of the street light, Victor found much to his dismay that Coco was not inside. Instead what he found was the partially butchered hind-quarters of a cow. A rotting sack of beef. He stopped digging and mashed the flattened cardboard boxes back on top of the pile. He lay down defeated, curled his arm up under his head like a pillow and closed his eyes. This only made the spinning worse. Victor retched all over his arm and spun into unconsciousness.

When Victor opened his eyes again, he was blinded by the sun. His ferocious hangover stabbed at the back of his eyes with disdain; pure hatred for every single ray of sunshine assaulting them. He threw his arm across his face. He heard the crunching of plastic bottles and the crinkling of papers beneath him. He lifted his arm an inch, and opened one eye. *Garbage. Great,* he thought, *I fell asleep in the dumpster.* He grumbled and rolled onto his back with his eyes still shut tight against the sun. It smelled worse than he remembered from the night before.

Victor braced himself for the brilliance of the sun and opened his eyes to see a perfect blue sky. He sat up on one arm. He looked around completely stunned. As far as he could see there was garbage. It stretched for miles in every direction. He was not in the dumpster anymore. He was at the dump. *I must have been out COLD when the garbage truck came.* He counted his blessings for having not been crushed en-route to the dump, and set off to find the entrance.

"Looks like I'll be spending money on cab fare after all," he muttered. Victor brushed some wilted lettuce from his hair and started walking.

Seven

The fly stopped crying.

Coco leaned as close to the orange as she could stomach. "I'm sorry I wrecked your house," she said. She meant it. At least she *thought* she meant it.

Coco was not the type of girl to go around destroying other people's things. She did once pour maple syrup into the air intake of an ex-boyfriend's truck, but she was nineteen and vindictive then, so it didn't really count. The fact that this was a fly's house, in some strange unconscious hallucination, didn't really make her feel any better.

The fly sat up, blew its nose into a section of orange peel and sniffled. "It isn't the house so much. I mean, sure, it's terrible to lose everything you own in one fell swoop." He briefly shot her a dirty look before sighing and continuing on. "It's just stuff. But I only have one week to live? I had a lot of things I wanted to do. Plans. Now what?" He slumped on his back four legs and let out a deep, exasperated sigh.

"I really am sorry." Coco extended her pinky finger to pat the fly on the head in an attempt to comfort the insect. "I've had quite the day myself."

The fly ducked under her finger. "Yeah, how's that?" he asked, straightening up.

"Well, I'm here," she said, indicating the dump.

"Big deal. Some people have real problems," the fly said, dismissing her. He buzzed over to the pile of his demolished personal effects next to his crushed aluminum home. He landed and surveyed the wreckage.

"No, really." Coco commiserated with the fly. She caught herself trying to converse and empathize with an insect, and

25

she realized how desperate she'd become for companionship. She had been roaming the landfill for most of the day talking to herself. It was nice to have another voice respond. Even if it was a fly's. "I was at work and something happened. I had an accident and I was electrocuted." She gestured to her matted fried hair. "When I woke up I was here. They just threw me away."

The fly nodded toward the silver high heels dangling from her hand. "Work, huh?" he scoffed.

Coco sat up straight and glared at the insect. "You know, it was an accident. I didn't know you lived in that can. And in fact you probably don't. You aren't even real. You are part of this dream I am having. And I don't *care* if you are mad at me. You're in my head."

The fly laughed and buzzed around her. "Did you hit your head, too? Lady, I'm just as real as you. As this dump." he shouted over his shoulder as he flew in a small circle a few feet away.

"Whatever. I just want to go home." she sighed.

The fly picked up a broken piece of furniture and examined it briefly. He turned it over before letting it fall back to the ground.

"At least you have a home," he said, defeated.

"But I don't know where it is. I don't know where I am, or how to get from here to there. Or what is wrong with me. Why am I talking to a fly?" Coco said standing up and shaking her head.

"Pity?" the fly said snidely.

Coco sighed. Whatever was going on didn't appear to be changing anytime soon.

"I really am sorry…fly."

"My name is Rudy."

"You have a *name*?"

"Of course I do. Don't you? Let me guess." Rudy buzzed around Coco's stilettos. "Crystal? Roxy? Candy?" Coco shook her head "no" with each name.

"You seem to have a problem with dancers, Rudy. I don't appreciate the attitude," she said when he had finished.

"I had an ex. She was a stripper. You hear me? STRIP-ER. None of this *dancer* shit. You didn't go to Juilliard. You're changing the subject. Whaddya call yourself?"

Coco was suddenly embarrassed. She stared at the shoes in her hand. "Coco. Coco Darling," she said.

Rudy snickered. "It could be worse. I once met a beastly woman who called herself *Niqueollette*," he said. He spelled the name. "What a train wreck that broad was."

"There's a strip club around here?" Coco asked brightly. If there was a strip club nearby there was sure to be someone who could drive her home. Or at least point her in the right direction.

"There used to be one in town, but the Queen had it condemned. I moved out here when the Queen banished all flies. I moved farther away than the others so I could live in peace for my final days." He cocked a fuzzy eyebrow at Coco. "But now I guess I have to head back. I can't just sleep in the wild."

"You can't?"

"No! Would you? Would you just go sleep in a prairie? Doubt it." Rudy started to buzz away.

"Wait! If you're heading to town…" Coco paused. "Are there only flies in this town?" For all she knew "town" was an empty six-pack a few yards from where she stood.

"It takes all kinds around here," Rudy said, looping through the air.

That was good enough for Coco. She followed him into the distant trashscape and hoped she would eventually find a way home.

Eight

Coco plodded along behind Rudy for some time. The ground finally became level.

The plastic wrapping around Coco's feet was tattered. She stopped to rest and strapped on her stilettos. Coco felt suddenly much more secure. She fished through a pile of trash. She was so hungry. She hoped there would be something she could eat without getting too ill. Like a Twinkie. Those things lasted forever. She knew she probably wouldn't be that blessed.

The longer Coco wandered the wasteland, and the more she got to know Rudy, the less she believed she was dreaming. Her dreams had never been this vivid or detailed. She couldn't recall ever having smelled a dream. Just as Coco began to weigh the possibility of having completely lost her mind, she unearthed a half eaten bag of trail mix from what appeared to be a crumpled mess of someone's study notes. She examined the bag briefly before tilting her head back and pouring the mix into her mouth. It tasted vaguely of rubbish. She was so hungry she hardly noticed it.

Rudy buzzed around Coco's head, exhausted. He landed in the mess of her hair, burrowed in and made himself a little nest of a bed.

Reclining and relaxing in her hair, Rudy said, "A little ways up, there is a hut. They may even let us stay the night. From there we can start fresh in the morning. Shouldn't be much farther now."

Normally Coco would find the mere thought of an insect making itself at home in her hair utterly repugnant. In this case, given that she had annihilated his home and he had still been so kind as to escort her to some kind of civilization, she made an exception. Besides, her hair was a mess already— stiff and fried from the electrocution. It had also begun to collect bits of paper, lint, and anything else the wind might have blown into it. Maybe this hut place would have a shower?

Excited by the prospect of cleanliness, Coco jumped to her feet and started off.

"Do you mind if I just take a nap here?" Rudy wheezed from her matted hair.

"Just don't lay any eggs in there." Coco cringed.

"I'm not making any promises." Rudy yawned and rolled over.

As Coco walked she could hear the faint sound of his teeny, tiny snoring.

Nine

Coco didn't notice that Rudy was awake until he landed on her nose. She could almost hear his small fuzzy smile as he said "Something smells exquisite!"

She wanted to believe him. He sounded so pleased with what he smelled. Whatever was creeping into her *own* nostrils made her eyes water. It smelled like the alley behind the club where Coco danced—the one that was shared with a butcher shop. She was glad, more than glad—relieved—that it was nearing dusk. She could only imagine what it must smell like around here at high-noon.

Coco stopped in her tracks. "What *is* that smell?"

Rudy pressed on, salivating. "We must be close to the Oracle now."

"The who?"

"This old woman. She can read your fortune. She's a strange old bat, but they say she sees things. Then they happen." Rudy shrugged four shoulders. "But they say a lot of things, don't they? For all I know she's just an old lady in a meat hut."

"MEAT hut?"

"She might be able to help you. It's worth a shot. Maybe we could even spend the night there!" Rudy's already globular eyes widened. He drooled.

"I don't know that I want to stay in anything called a *meat hut*." Coco winced.

Rudy looked back at her as he followed the enticing stench. "Said the stripper who did *what* exactly with sausage?"

"Brautwurst." Coco scowled. She knew she shouldn't

have told him that.

She followed him reluctantly, feeling insulted. As they neared the Oracle, Coco continued to ponder what in the hell a meat hut could possibly be. And the stench got stronger.

By the time they could see the hut, the smell was unbearable. Coco's stomach lurched. Rudy was leaving an alarmingly obvious trail of slobber in his wake. It dropped into the air after him and landed like a fine mist across Coco's forearm as she walked behind him. She kept trying to switch sides, or just walk a bit slower or faster, but Rudy never flew in a straight line. He made loops and swirls and zig-zags, all the while intoxicated by the vile aroma.

Coco and Rudy stopped in front of the house. Coco tried to pinch her nose to avoid smelling it, but breathing through her mouth she could almost TASTE it; rotting meat. She cupped a hand over her nose and mouth in an attempt to find some happy medium and walked up to the front door.

The hut was a small aluminum structure bent into a roundish shape and bound with baling wire. The roof of the hut was shingled with thick slabs of decaying meat, writhing and squirming with maggots. There were black patches vibrating with the buzz of flies.

Rudy quickly scanned the crowd and ducked back into Coco's mangled mane.

"Friends? Enemies? Ex-lovers?" Coco laughed as she shook a finger through her tangled hair where Rudy hid, mocking him.

"Shut up." Rudy hissed.

"Why not go say hello?" Coco pried.

"I don't want them to know that I am dying. They can't know how sick I am," he whispered.

"This illness you have," Coco said, through her fingers "It isn't contagious, is it?"

"I don't think so. When the Queen banished the flies, we all came here. I slipped inside to visit the Oracle one day. She took one look at me and said 'You're going to die in a week.' When I asked her what kind of illness I had, or what was going to happen to me, all she said was 'This is the way these things happen.'"

"Great." Coco dropped the subject as Rudy had already been living in her hair and on parts of her face for the bulk of the day.

Coco reached the front step and gagged. In place of a door was a curtain made from the intestines of some small animal. They were nailed to the wooden door frame, and hung like a beaded curtain—only instead of beads, ropes of thick, vein-riddled, rotting guts swayed in the putrid wind. Coco's stomach lurched.

Coco knocked on the wooden door frame with her free hand. The wood was soft and damp with rotting intestinal fluid that had rubbed into the wood. She smeared her hand against the side of her leg trying to wipe away the wetness. Since her dress was made of plastic bags, most of the gunk just smeared across the back of her hand and wrist.

"Ugh. Hello?" Coco called through her hands. She heard the creak of a chair shifting underneath someone's weight, followed by soft shuffling footsteps.

Knobby skeleton fingers wrapped in thin, paper-white skin slid through the gut curtain. They curled around a piece of the draped entrails and pulled it aside, leaving a gap barely large enough for someone to peer outside. Only the hand could be seen beyond the shadows of the meat hut.

"What?" croaked a voice through the stench.

Coco was not sure how much more of the odor she could tolerate. She tried to breathe through the gaps between her fingers to filter the smell, but when she inhaled it attacked her senses full force. "I seem to be lost," Coco said, trying not to gag.

"Seems so," croaked the voice, "no one comes around here on purpose."

"I can see why."

"But folks end up here for a reason. So you may as well come in. I'll see what they have to say about you."

Coco was confused. "They?"

"Come on in. I'll make some tea." Bony fingers curled under stained shirt-sleeves, hanging like potato sacks around dainty, frail wrists, gesturing for her to come inside.

Coco could only imagine what could possibly be inside the meat hut. The stench was tremendously appalling outside, even at a distance. She'd already nearly vomited at least three times. *Inside* the hut? She thought she might revisit the trail mix she'd eaten. And it wasn't exactly delectable the first time.

Ten

The hand disappeared inside. The voice said, "Please, come in. I'll put the kettle on."

Coco heard slow, shambling footsteps drifting deeper inside the hut. She stood on the porch and breathed into the palm of her hand repeatedly. She stared at the curtain but did not make a move to enter.

"It's not solid," the voice said, "you can just walk right through. It'll move."

Coco could not figure a way of entering the hut without touching the intestines. She took a deep breath for courage and immediately regretted it.

She slowly reached for the gut-curtain. As her hand got closer, she realized she was really going to have to walk through the intestines. *Just think of it like the car wash.* She closed her eyes and slid her hand between two slick strips. They felt spongy and moist against her arm. *Just like the car wash*, she thought. She tried to picture her favorite car wash back home. Soapy. Sudsy. Clean. She played these images to herself like a movie behind closed eyelids as she stepped forward.

Holding the innards to one side, away from her face, Coco jumped into the meat hut. A long, pink intestinal tendril slipped around her outstretched hand and slapped her across the face. It left viscous goo clinging to her skin. She gasped, trying not to scream, so as to not offend her hostess. Even if the old woman lived in a rotting meat hut, Coco still believed in manners. The possibility of vomiting also struck Coco as rude. She wondered how the Oracle managed to live like this.

Coco looked around the hut. Most of the light in the small room came from the sun shining between gaps in its aluminum walls, though a few small candles on a table across the room provided some. The fire under the kettle mostly just made shadows on the bumpy aluminum. Coco figured it was probably for the best that it was fairly dark. With too much light, she might be forced to focus on the ceiling—which was clearly made of meat.

She could hear blood and bits of meat drip to the floor. Now and then, a small drop would splash on her arm. It was at this point that she ruled out all possibility of taking a shower. Perhaps it should have occurred to her sooner, but with a snoutful of rotting flesh, it was difficult to focus.

The old woman shuffled around some small glass jars near the kettle. Each one was filled with different colored herbs, liquids, or strange gelatinous blobs. Something squirmy shifted in a few of them when the firelight caused shadows to stretch and undulate. The contents of those jars seemed to hunger for the dark, pressing to the blackest glass.

Her hostess ambled around the table. She set tea for two: two tea cups, each a different color—one a solid slate gray and the other white with tiny peach-colored roses lining the rim. Both of the cups were chipped. The grey one had a moderately visible crack that stretched from its base all around the handle.

The saucers for each cup were robin's egg blue with a delicate daisy hand-painted in the center. The woman set out a bowl of sugar cubes which looked pretty normal. While the Oracle was making their tea, Rudy darted from his hiding place in Coco's hair and landed in the sugar bowl. When he took flight again at least three cubes were missing.

The old woman lifted the large iron kettle from the fire. She poured hot water into a round-bellied clay pot—which was in dire need of a glaze. Coco figured it must be older than the woman, who turned to Coco, holding it up for her to see. It was the first time Coco had gotten a good look at her. Before then the woman had been a pile of faded black fabric gliding across the hut with the choppy movement of a stormy sea.

She must have been a hundred. Her eyes were sunken deep into their sockets and coated a milky white. Her hair was a thin tuft of white feathers poking sporadically from her liver-spotted pale scalp. Her bony hands moved shakily about the table as she prepared her own cup of tea. "Do you take milk?" she asked Coco as she poured from a small pitcher into her own cup.

The milk plopped into her tea in chunks. She stirred it vigorously; the spoon clinked against the cracked ceramic until the lumps had mostly dissolved. A thin layer of solidified milk particles remained floating atop the old woman's tea like mini marshmallows in hot chocolate.

"No, thank you. In fact I'm not really all that thirsty," she said, eyeing the tea pot. Lord knew what was brewing in there.

"Oh, please. Have just one cup with me. It's so soothing. And then we can get to whatever it is that has brought you here." The old woman handed the teapot to Coco with rickety hands. The lid clattered against the pot with her trembling.

Coco accepted the pot, lifted the lid, and peered inside. It actually smelled good—like orange blossoms and jasmine. The delicious floral scent was a shock to her senses after spending her entire day surrounded by a rotting trash heap. She inhaled deeply and closed her eyes.

"See? Soothing," the old woman said, raising her grey cup. She slurped at the hot liquid and put the cup down. Her hand shuddered and it clinked against the saucer several times before she unwound her spindly fingers from the handle.

Coco held her own cup of tea an inch from her face and breathed heavily, relishing the sweet delicate scent. "Yes, it is." She took a long slow sip. Then another. She had not realized how thirsty she was. Coco set the cup to rest atop its daisy-printed saucer and looked up at the old woman who was gazing into her tea. "I hear you are an oracle. That you see things, and that you might be able to help me get home."

The Oracle put her cup down and settled back into her

chair. "I may be able to, yes. I can make no promises. I only see what is shown to me."

Coco picked up the teapot and looked under the lid again, savoring the smell of the fresh brewed herbs. "Do you read tea leaves?" she asked.

"Oh no, I practice a much older form of divination. Its roots run deeper." The old woman rose from her seat and shambled over to a hutch against the wall. "Here, let me show you."

"Tarot cards? Or those little rocks with the stick figures on them?" Coco asked.

"No." The Oracle wheezed as she hefted a large burlap sack onto the table. "Flesh."

Eleven

Coco sat stunned and still. The old lady squished a large, sodden burlap sack onto the table.

"Wouldn't you rather just read my palm?" Coco asked, extending her open hand to the Oracle.

"Not at all. Hands lie. Living tissue lies. It has a will of its own. And the lines of a hand are so limited. They have no character. There is nothing to read but the way a line is frayed, and where it is placed." The Oracle jostled the bag on the table and the meats inside made cold, damp sounds while strange colored fluids seeped from the seams of the bag.

Coco returned her teacup to its position in front of her face.

The Oracle continued, "Meat is multi-faceted. Which part of a creature it comes from is just as important as any symbol you might find on a tarot card or a rune stone, or the shape that tea leaves make, settled on the bottom of your cup. The advancement of the decay can tell you so much. Its aroma and texture speak volumes." The old woman rolled her sleeve up to her elbow and thrust an emaciated arm into the sack. She swirled it around, stirring the meat about in the bag with bare hands.

Coco looked on, eyes wide with shock and disgust.

"While I cannot provide you with a map home, I can provide you with a few pieces of information from the Powers. Things that may not make sense now, but will help you along your journey." The Oracle looked up from the bag at Coco and stopped mid-churn."That is, unless you don't want my help."

Coco sat watching the ancient woman, up to her elbows

in rotten flesh, speechless and uncertain.

"If not, you may enjoy your cup of tea and be on your way. But the draw here," the Oracle said, as she continued to churn the meat with her hand, "is strong. There are things they want you to know. It would be a shame not to listen."

Coco let out a small sigh. It was not as though she had many options. There hadn't been another human around for the whole day and Coco was a sucker for a touch of mysticism.

"I'd like to know what they know," Coco said. She put her cup on the table beside the bag. "I don't have to touch it do I?"

"Not if you don't want to." The Oracle breathed deeply and closed her eyes. She began to hum as she fished around in the bag.

"How does this work?"

"I feel for what needs to be shown. The energy will call to me and I will choose that piece. Now kindly shut your mouth while I concentrate."

Coco sat back in her chair watching the old woman work. She whirled her hands through the bag and fished out seven objects which she slapped down on the table in front of Coco. Each piece splashed as it collided with the solid surface of the table.

The Oracle opened her eyes and evaluated each item on the table in silence. Her face bore an expression of puzzlement.

"What is it?" Coco asked. The Oracle's intense contemplation was making Coco uneasy.

The old woman gestured to the objects laid out in a straight, gooey line across the table. "It's like a timeline. First, we have this bit of brain here." She held a gray blob between her skeletal index finger and thumb. She pressed it gently and its casing gave way like pudding skin. It oozed a thick yellow cream that looked like custard. "It signifies confusion. Bewilderment."

Coco laughed. "Yeah, I'd say that's pretty accurate."

Next the Oracle picked up a long strand of red tissue.

"This muscle…" She dangled it in the air in front of her face like a child eating spaghetti, and sniffed it. The old woman wound the sinewy muscle around her bony fingers. "It usually indicates an adventure. Some kind of travel."

"Look, you're not telling me anything I don't already know."

The Oracle held up her hand, motioning for Coco's silence. She picked up a toe and turned it over in her hand. Picking at the nail bed and examining the inside. "This generally signifies danger. A small one," she said, waving the toe in the air like a mother would waggle a finger at their child. "So, tread lightly." She snickered, pleased with her own pun as she set it back on the table.

Coco pushed herself away from the table. "Wait just a fucking minute. This bag is full of human parts?"

"Partially, yes. It's a rich medley really," the Oracle said, nuzzling the burlap. "Ah…." She reached over and picked up a small dark brown glob. "This liver means that the danger will pass."

The old woman kneaded the liver in her hands before placing it back on the table, which left her fingers stained with the faintest shade of olive green.

"Ew," Coco whispered.

"Oh, but this. This gem…" The Oracle picked up a tubular chunk and held it to the candlelight, peering through it like a telescope. "This is a heart valve. It means there is a great love in your very near future."

Coco grinned.

"But it has a vegetation." The old woman held it out for Coco to see. The inside of the valve was dense with what looked like filthy cauliflower. "It means there will be a great many complications.

Coco's grin slipped slowly down her face until she was pouting. "Hmph." She snorted and crossed her arms. There always were.

"Oh my. This is very rare." The Oracle moved slowly to the other side of the table.

She did not reach for the eyeball that had been staring

at Coco throughout the entire reading as Coco had hoped she would. It was not only giving her the willies, but she was dying to know what it meant. The Oracle reached for something that Coco had overlooked in the barrage of organs flung from the sack onto the table. She reached for a small, battered dandelion with a long wispy stem. It hung limp and heavy with blood and other fluids.

"A flower," Coco said cheerfully. "Well, that must be something good. Perhaps my prince and I will overcome those complications." She bounced in her chair. That would be a welcomed first. Many times before, Coco had sought out love and failed. Miserably.

"On the contrary, it means great loss and suffering. It can mean grave danger as well. This is not to be taken lightly." The Oracle spun the dandelion between her fingers by its stem and examined it closely. She inhaled deeply at its center, contemplating the scent. Then she licked the petals clean. "You must prepare for a great loss, dear girl. Larger than you have ever known."

"What is going to happen? Will I be okay?" Coco asked, alarmed by the Oracle's warning.

"Unfortunately I cannot tell you. The final item of this reading is the eye." She picked it up by its long string of nerves and veins and let it dangle before Coco like a pendulum. "The eye signifies the unknowable. Something too hazy to be seen. Blindness. Your outcome is unclear."

"That can't be all. You can't sit here and tell me how much danger I am about to be in and then *not* tell me how it turns out." Coco stood and stamped her foot.

"But I can. In fact, that's all I *can* do," the Oracle said calmly.

"There isn't, like, a follow-up portion? A bonus round? *Something?*"

"I'm afraid not. But nothing is written in stone. At least you have been warned. Consider yourself lucky for that. Some do not get that luxury."

"Luxury? You think it's a luxury to be told that something really fucking awful is about to happen to me? What am I going to lose? What kind of danger will I be in?" Coco was having trouble breathing. She sat down at the table again.

"Some people do not get a warning." The Oracle wiped her hands on the inside of her faded robe.

Coco could see the crusted, filthy material inside, stained from many readings past—other warnings of love, danger and death. She hoped that maybe some were happier and less open-ended.

The Oracle said, "I do not know what you are going to lose. It may be your love, your life, yourself. It could be anything, really. You won't know what it is until it's gone."

"Well, that's just fucking great." Coco stood up from the table, placing her hands palms-down on the surface. "Thanks for the tea, I guess. Can you point me towards town?"

The Oracle raised an arm. Her sleeve was still rolled up and bits of meat goo streaked her nearly translucent skin. "It's half a day's walk from here, at least. And it is getting late. If you'd like, I could fix up a guest bed. You haven't had a good night's rest until you've slept on a mattress stuffed with meat. It contours to your body perfectly and it absorbs heat. It's like being back in the womb." The Oracle closed her eyes dreamily and held her hands in the prayer position over her heart.

"Thanks but I had better be on my way." She slipped across the room and wriggled her way back through the intestine curtain delicately, trying to get past with as little skin-to-guts contact as possible.

Coco stood outside the Oracle's meat hut staring out at the vast expanse of refuse and potential doom that lay before her. A pair of rats stopped and blinked their beady eyes at her before scuttling away. Somewhere out there something was waiting to harm her. If she *could* be harmed here. She still wanted to believe that she was coma-dreaming, but found that rather difficult.

Rudy landed on her nose. He hadn't been in her hair.

"Where did you go?"

"It was getting heavy in there," he said.

"Yeah, tell me about it."

"And it was making me hungry. All that meat just lying around. So I left. How did it go?"

"Not well." Coco pouted. She looked out over the landscape. The sun was setting and there was a chill in the light breeze. She shivered and thought of a love she had not yet met, but would soon lose. "We should probably get moving. I don't suppose there is a hotel around here?"

Rudy laughed and buzzed away while Coco followed him. They traveled until the sky was black. They found a pile of wooden pallets with an old torn mattress perched on top. It had a few brownish stains and springs poked through the fabric here and there. Coco curled up on the mattress and stared up at the sky. She couldn't remember the last time she had seen the stars. Or the last time she hadn't been on stage at night. She closed her eyes and drifted off to sleep.

Twelve

The sun beat heavily on Coco when she awoke. She could feel sweat pooling inside her plastic garment. She was wholly disappointed to find that she was, in fact, still at the dump.

She sat up and looked around. "Well, fuck…"

Rudy buzzed over from a pile of rotting food where he had been feasting. He looped around her head and weaved around her arms. "You smell delightful."

Coco doubted that very much. She longed for the sweetness of her favorite cotton candy-scented body spray. She rose slowly and spent a few moments stretching her long body like a feline. She was delighted to see a pile of discarded clothing nearby. She dug through it for something to wear.

Almost all of the clothing seemed to have been damaged in a fire. The fabric crumbled in her hand when she touched it. The only article that was somewhat salvageable was a singed bridesmaid's dress. A pink one. It had tiers of ruffles, and a large scalloped sash that cut across the chest. It was dreadful.

Coco unwound the plastic bags from her body. Small streams of sweat poured over her breasts, and down her torso and legs. She stood naked for a moment and let the breeze dry and cool her before she slipped into the pink ruffled monstrosity.

"Always the bridesmaid," she said.

The dress tightly hugged her frame. It had cheap plastic boning in the bodice which pushed her breasts up in perfect mounds and stabbed at her ribcage. She shook the neckline of the dress vigorously from side to side to adjust her cleavage.

There was a section running up from the base of the dress that had been burned out completely and left a large gap up the side. Coco's leg was exposed almost to the hip.

Rudy landed there and paced the charred fabric with three sets of rapid feet. "This part sort of smells like bacon..."

"Bacon? Why would the dress smell like bacon?" Coco asked.

"Because someone was probably still wearing it when it caught on fire."

Coco looked down at the dress in horror but realized that she had few options. It was this or stifling plastic. "Fuck it," she said and began walking again.

They traveled for hours until they came to a large crumbling stone barrier and a rusty wrought iron gate. A small wooden shack stood to the right of the gate. Its planks were crumbling with dry-rot. Large sections of its walls were missing, which made it more like a lean-to or a booth.

Coco and Rudy approached a large, cracked cashier's window at the front of the structure. It seemed silly to Coco to have to use a window when there were so many places along the sides to just step right through.

"Hello?" Coco called. There was no response. No shuffling or creaking. Not a single sound of life inside. She knocked on the window. The glass rattled against the pane, but otherwise, there were no sounds.

She walked around the side of the building and peered through a hole in the wall. No one was inside, and the room was completely empty. Weeds had grown between the floorboards. Coco stepped inside and the wood splintered underneath her weight. She tumbled gracelessly to the floor.

Rudy laughed.

She stood up and dusted herself off, feeling foolish. Clearly, no one was inside the building. She stepped back through the hole in the wall. She heard a low, mechanical whirring sound outside—like gears or fans—some kind of machinery. She couldn't make out just what it was.

Coco followed the sound to the outside corner of the house. With each step it got louder. She stopped before she turned the corner, suddenly afraid of what she might find. Deciding she had to see what it was, Coco rounded the building. Her ears were assaulted with a shrieking "BEEEEP!! BEEEEP! BEEEEEP! BEEEEP!"

Coco jumped back startled and flattened herself against the wall with such force that the entire section let out a low miserable groan and collapsed behind her.

Thirteen

Coco lay flat on her back atop a pile of rust-colored wood. A large dust cloud rose, leaving her unable to see what came toward her—whirring, beeping and grinding. A large shadow loomed out of the dust, blurry at first, but becoming clearer as it approached. It appeared to be a robot—a terribly disorganized robot—and as it got closer she began to be able to decipher its construction.

It had a small round object for a head, which looked like it was jammed on a spike and driven into its bulky, square body. Its boxy torso had a smaller glowing square in its center. Two long arms waved from its sides. Two crazy legs were attached in such a way that caused the robot to walk in uneven, awkward steps.

When it was closer, Coco saw that the robot's head was something from her childhood—the rounded chubby face of a Cabbage Patch Kid. Its hair had all been torn out except for a few small tufts of ragged yarn. Small holes littered the scalp. A metal antenna stuck through the center of its ragged plastic skull. A red light flashed at the antenna's tip. Coco could see that the robot's black square torso was a huge, industrial microwave.

The microwave beeped furiously. The LCD screen scrolled "FINISHED" in flashing green letters. Coco scrambled to her feet, and the thing moved toward her through the plume of filth.

One of the robot's arms was a long piece of PVC pipe with a hand mixer attached to the end. The spinning mixer was aimed at Coco who stood staring, paralyzed with fear. The machine began to shoot red and white projectiles with tiny flapping tails from its mixer arm.

It wasn't until one of them hit Coco that she realized they were tampons. Used tampons. She screamed and turned to run. The robot jumped forward and grabbed her by the hair with what Coco saw was a human arm. It was the gray, bloodless color of a lifeless limb, but it was muscular. Coco would have admired its well-sculpted muscles were they not attached to a gross, recycled arm trying to snap her bones through her skin.

The machine continued its furious blending. It brought the blender closer and closer to Coco's head, and although the spokes were not sharp enough to cut her, she screamed all the same. The machine continued to beep. It caught Coco's hair in the mixer and pulled it tight.

Tugging free meant tearing away a large portion of her scalp. But letting the monstrous robot keep ahold of her seemed worse. Coco pulled and struggled against the machine, screaming for someone to help her.

The mixer whirred, tightening its grip. The microwave beeped. Coco could see a tampon stuck behind the mixer blades, twisting as they spun. From the corner of her eye, she saw the human arm reaching to the machine's microwave chest. It opened the door while the mixer arm pulled her closer. The robot punched in numbers on the keypad and tried to shove Coco's head inside. The human arm, with its fleshy, gray fingers punching buttons, reached for the START button.

Coco screamed while the machine shoved her head inside the microwave. Her own shrieks nearly deafened her—bouncing off of the inside of the box. She closed her eyes tight and waited for a pile of bubbling goo to replace her face, kicking and pounding on the junky killing machine killing her.

She wondered if the door had to be closed to nuke her head. Part of her hoped so, but part of her knew that meant decapitation was a possibility.

As she twisted against the mixer tearing her hair, and its hard plastic arm holding her head inside the microwave,

Coco felt another hand grasp the back of her dress and yank her backward. She heard the sound of metal scraping on metal as she flew back with her eyes squeezed closed.

Coco landed on all fours and crawled away on shaky knees through sludge and soggy paper products as quickly as she could manage. She turned her head and looked back over her shoulder. She saw the broad back of a man wielding a machete. He tossed his weapon inside the microwave, slammed the door and punched the START button.

The robot's doll head had the eyes of a sad puppy painted-on plastic on an otherwise expressionless face. Despite its communicative handicap, the machine's panic was obvious. It turned left, then right, then left again. It groped desperately at the microwave door with its mixer hand. Its dead human arm squirmed in the dirt at its feet.

Blue sparks danced inside the machine's microwave chest and the timer ticked off the numbers: 7, 6, 5, 4… More sparks spurted from the vents on the machine's side.It sputtered and shook, convulsing and sparking above Coco as she cowered behind a small pile of goop.

The man dove on top of her, tackling her flat to the ground and covering her body with his. Coco's face was pressed into the dirt. Rotten juices and soggy particles of who-knows-what seeped between her lips. She closed her eyes tighter and tried not to swallow while she heard the machine beeping in panic. Then there was a roaring explosion, and metal and plastic clattered to the ground around her.

When the sound of raining mechanical remains sputtered to a stop, Coco noticed that the man was still crushing her into the soggy disgusting ground. She wriggled around beneath him for a while, before saying "Would you mind getting the fuck off of me?"

Coco stood and shook the debris from her dress and hair. She reached up and shook her hand through her matted tresses. She found a good hunk of hair had been cut off. The man had chopped it with his machete to free her from the mixer. She wanted to be angry, but despite her lopsided and matted hairdo, she was alive and not being cooked in a microwave. So she thanked him instead.

"It's my job to maintain the Gatekeeper," he said. He moved wreckage to retrieve his weapon. "It's been malfunctioning lately. They only perform for so long before they get a little crazy. Sorry I didn't get here sooner." He looked at the ground sheepishly.

"I'd say you got here just in time." Coco offered.

She looked him over. He was a tall, broad man. He wore full body armor made from tires. The tread neatly lined up and looked like stylish utilitarian pin-striping. He had a rugged look about him. It could have been the tire tread body armor, his scruffy, unshaven face and unkempt hair, the tattoos peeking up out of his collar and crawling across the exposed flesh of his stubbly neck. Coco didn't care much one way or the other. He had saved her life and he was delicious.

Fourteen

"What are you doing on this side of the gate anyway?" the rugged rubber-clad man asked Coco.

"Waiting for you?" Coco said coyly with a wink.

"Cute," the man said. He was obviously not impressed. "You could be in a lot of trouble for leaving the kingdom. Did you get a pass?"

Coco could see that her usual games and flirtation would get her nowhere. She would have to resort to being herself. After years on the stage and telling men what they wanted to hear for their measly dollars, she wasn't even sure who that was, but was left with little other choice.

"I woke up here. I mean, not *here*. I've been traveling for a day or so. I woke up a ways from here and the Oracle pointed me this way."

"You've seen the Oracle?" The man looked at her with surprise floating somewhere within his mysterious blue eyes. Coco found it hard to focus when he looked at her.

"Yeah, she told me that—"

The man held up his hand, "I don't want to know. The things she tells you are between you and her. No one else."

Coco shot a look at Rudy who was buzzing around gawking at the wreckage of the Gatekeeper.

Rudy shrugged. "Sue me for being curious. But I left, didn't I? I didn't hear the whole reading."

The man looked at Rudy and then back to Coco. "You let him stay?"

"Well, no. Not exactly. I mean, I didn't know that no one else was supposed to know what she told me. And like he said, he left before she finished." Coco stammered. She

51

hated that he made her so nervous. He was different from the men she knew. Not just because he wore a rubber suit, or possibly lived in a landfill, but the way that he carried himself—secure, confident, and with a sense of purpose. She felt she could melt right where she stood. "I'm just trying to find my way home."

"And where might that be?"

"NOT in a landfill?"

"A what?"

"A place like this. Filled with trash?"

He stared at her blankly.

"Forget it. My name is Coco," she said. She extended her hand with poise, which he took, but did not kiss as she had hoped.

"Adrian," he said perfunctorily. He grasped her hand firmly and gave it a good shake.

"Can you take me to this kingdom of yours? Maybe someone there can help me?" She batted her eyelashes.

Adrian turned and began to march away. Coco stood and watched him. She looked over at Rudy, who just shrugged and began to follow Adrian.

"Come on then," Adrian called over his shoulder, "it's nearly dinner time at the palace. And, personally, I am famished."

Directly inside the gate sat a pile of decrepit Gatekeepers. They were sad looking, defunct robots, rusted in a heap consisting of a washing machine, a vacuum cleaner, some roller skates, a television set, two pairs of garden shears and a set of crutches. A mass grave for the former guardians of the kingdom. Coco paused to survey the mess and raised an inquisitive eyebrow at Adrian.

"Like I said, sometimes they get out of hand. Come on."

Adrian led Coco down a path where the trash had been shoveled to either side. They came to a bubbling puddle of greenish goo.

Coco stopped walking. "What is that?"

Adrian smiled brightly. "The pond. You should see it in the moonlight. It's really very lovely."

"I'm sure." Coco tried to hide the look of disgust smeared all over her face. Dead goldfish floated on the surface and insects crawled in and out of the goo. Their bodies were coated in an oil-slick sheen. Mountains of trash towered over them. In the distance, some were topped with paper products. If Coco squinted she could pretend they were snow capped peaks.

There was a park with jagged playground equipment deemed unsafe for children years ago. Yet here, the children in their patchwork rags played and screamed gleefully. A tree in the center of the park dripped with tire swings and dirty, happy children. Their mothers stared cautiously at Coco as she and Adrian walked to the center of the village. Rudy felt a bit ragged and decided to nap the rest of the way to the castle, tucked in the folds of Coco's over-puffed dress sleeve.

They passed strange dwellings constructed from old tires, wood, and large bricks of compacted waste. Several of the doors had holes large enough to crawl through and the windows were mostly just holes cut raggedly into the trash bricks.

Coco asked Adrian many questions. At first he answered in brief one word responses. But soon he relaxed and became more comfortable conversing with Coco. She learned that he was a knight, but primarily worked as a maintenance man for the Queen. It was his job to repair things like the Gatekeeper, the gate itself, and any other item the Queen felt needed an adjustment.

"Lately, since she is in heat, the Queen will just call a group of the knights to her quarters to check for loose floorboards. I usually find a way out of it, like claiming I am already on a repair. Especially now that the spores are dropping." Adrian shuddered.

"Spores, like mold? Your queen is human, right?" Coco asked.

"She is *mostly* human, but yes, like mold. Now that she is in the late stages of this mating cycle, she drops spores. They are meant to attract a mate to her. Essentially by force."

"Does it work?"

"She's had three husbands since I have served here, all under the influence of her spores. She eventually grows bored and has them sent to the Chamber. Then the next cycle begins and she starts all over again."

"What is the Chamber?" Coco asked, linking arms with him.

Adrian smiled down at her. She adored his rare yet brilliant smile. "Let's just hope you never find out."

Fifteen

The castle was a large pair of glass towers at the center of town. Some sections were filled with alternating green and blue glass bottles. They gave the vague impression of stained glass. The sun shone through the bottles, lighting the ground below blue and green. The two towers were joined by two sections of wall and a gate between them.

Adrian reached for the door and stopped. He pointed at a sign printed in large bold letters:

STOP! NO FLIES ALLOWED!

Coco read the sign aloud and looked at Rudy, who was awake but still nestled in the pink shoulder of her frock. "You may have to wait out here."

"I'll just hide in your sleeve. Maybe your hair. They'll never know I am here. I won't make a sound," Rudy pled.

Coco looked at Adrian like a little girl begging for a puppy.

"The Queen won't like it. She won't tolerate it." He shook his head.

"But if she doesn't know..."

Adrian took a deep breath. He released the air slowly, like a human tire that had sprung a leak. "Fine. But! If she should discover him, I knew nothing of it."

He pulled the door open and the smell of roasting meat

hit Coco square in the face. For a moment, her mind drifted to the Oracle and her bag of meaty fortunes, but her hunger took over and her stomach began to growl. She stepped inside and Adrian shut the door behind her.

The Queen's servants were sharing their evening meal in a large courtyard. Long planks of wood held up by barrels were covered in plate after plate of roasted meat. Servants sat on boxes, old broken chairs with wobbly, lopsided legs, and stacks of old phone books.

Adrian pulled out a gray-white, cracked plastic patio chair mostly comprised of duct tape. "You can have my seat, I'll go and find another." He smiled at Coco, but once he looked up at the other servants of the court his face went back to stone. All business. He marched off through a door to retrieve another chair for himself.

The servants in the courtyard appeared to be knights like Adrian. They all wore similar rubber armor, and greeted Coco with warm smiles. She took Adrian's seat happily and the knight to her left handed her a plate. Coco reached out and grabbed three slabs of meat from the platter in front of her. Two of them she slapped down on her plate, and the third she bit into directly.

The other knights had no silverware so she was not all too concerned with proper table etiquette. She dug into the meat like a rabid animal, letting the juices dribble down her chin and onto the front of her dress. After several bites, she noticed a few of the knights staring at her. She put the slab of meat down and wiped her mouth with her dress. Then she tore small pieces from the roasted meat and placed them in her mouth, which she kept closed while she chewed.

Adrian returned with a wooden crate and squeezed beside her. He grabbed a few slices of meat.

The man beside him held up a slab, tore it into strips and let juice run down his arms. He looked over at Coco, who had her mouth rather full. "Have you ever tasted feline so tender?" he asked.

Coco stopped mid-chew. She managed to yell through her mouthful, "Excuse me?!"

"The cat," the knight said. He held up a strip of roasted meat and waved it around. "It's extra delicious this evening. It seems you showed up on the right night!" He grinned at Coco, with pieces of shredded cat wedged between his yellow teeth.

Coco leaned forward and spit the wad of meat onto her plate. The others watched her, stunned.

Adrian raised an eyebrow "Is there something wrong?"

"You're damned right there's something wrong! I'm eating CAT?! Why the fuck are you people eating cats?!" She spat onto her plate in an attempt to get any and all particles of cat meat out of her mouth.

"What do you mean—" Adrian started to ask. But he was cut off by a lofty, inquisitive voice from down the table.

"Is there a problem?"

Coco looked along the rows of knights toward the voice, ready to fire off comments about how wrong and barbaric it was to eat cute fuzzy kittens, but when she saw who spoke, she quickly rethought her strategy. "No. No problem. I'm just full."

The Queen said, "I see. And just who might YOU be?"

Coco needn't ask who was inquiring. The Queen wore an elaborate barbed wire crown encrusted with shiny bits of broken costume jewelry. Her dress flowed with layers of old bed sheets and curtains—solids, florals, plaids. But it was her face that drew the most attention.

Half her face was that of any pale, middle-aged woman's. There were some wrinkles around her mouth, crow's feet, and three deep lines that cracked through her forehead from furrowing her brow. The other half of her face was fitted with a piece of metal mesh, molded to form the structure of a human head. Instead of a left eye, she had a forty-watt light bulb. It blinked off and on when she spoke. She wore her hair in an elaborate orange and white twist that sat atop her head like a delicious pastry. Coco found this very distracting.

Adrian answered for Coco and himself while she stared. He stood at his place at the table and spoke with diligent respect and clarity, "Your highness, this woman is a traveler and she—"

The Queen interrupted him. "Adrian," she said breathily, "since when do we take in strays? Except to eat them." Her smile stretched wide, her teeth sharp, metallic points, and she laughed haughtily.

The other servants joined in laughing.

It wasn't until the boom of laughter around her that Coco realized that everyone at the table was male, save herself and the Queen.

"Continue!" the Queen barked once the din of laughter had faded.

Adrian gathered himself and explained that Coco had woken up not far from the kingdom and needed help getting home. He started confidently, but under the scrutiny of the Queen, he wavered. Coco watched him struggle to gain composure.

"So," the Queen sighed heavily, "You've brought an outsider to my kingdom?" She crossed her arms over her chest and squinted disapproval at Adrian.

He opened his mouth to argue. Coco could see that he obviously did not want to displease the Queen. He looked to Coco, and then back down the table with wanting eyes. Then he bowed his head in submission and uttered a simple, "Yes, your Majesty."

"I see," the Queen said. "I would ask you why…" Adrian looked up with a faint glimmer of hope in his eyes. The monarch continued, "but I know quite well that the answer is *stupidity*. Now take your seat. I'll deal with you after dinner."

Sixteen

After a stony end to dinner, Coco and Adrian stood and waited for the other knights to say their goodbyes to the Queen. They bowed low, giving praise. Coco watched each knight bend down and kiss the Queen's hand before exiting. Coco could see small pebbles pop off the Queen's dress each time a knight kissed her hand. Some landed on the floor and rolled around listlessly, while the next knight side-stepped them or tried to crush them under his large black rubber boot.

"What are those things?" Coco whispered to Adrian.

"Spores," he whispered back as one launched onto the neck of a knight who'd lingered just a bit too long.

The knight stood, oblivious to the spore. As he passed Coco, she saw the purplish blob throb and pulsate on the knight's neck. He walked through a door, and turned to smile with the sweetest of adoration at the Queen. He stared longingly at her and she waved coyly at him while he blew a kiss at her.

"I guess they do work," Coco snickered to herself.

Adrian looked at her sheepishly. He didn't seem to find any amusement in the situation.

"Adrian," the Queen called out to him. "Come and speak with me. Bring your stray along."

"My name is Coco."

"I do not recall addressing it, Adrian. Tell it not to speak to me." The Queen rolled her head back and gazed at the ceiling, nose in the air.

"Please refrain from addressing the Queen unless she has acknowledged you specifically," Adrian said. His voice was firm.

Coco did not enjoy being spoken to in this way. Nor did she relish the idea of the two of them having a conversation about her as though she weren't standing right in front of them.

"Good night, Adrian." The Queen extended her hand and smiled a shiny, silver smile.

Adrian bowed on one knee as the other knights had, and pressed his closed mouth to her pale hand.

Coco stood behind him with her arms crossed, glaring at the Queen, who stared directly into her eyes over the top of Adrian's head. She gave Coco a mean little crooked smile and wriggled in her seat for a moment before she bounced, ever-so-slightly.

The Queen did not break eye contact with Coco while she released another small purple orb. It made a small arc, and Coco watched in horror as it planted itself firmly on the back of Adrian's head.

"No!" Coco reached out to grab the pulsating thing latched to the back of Adrian's head. The Queen clapped loudly and two guards appeared from the door behind her seat. They rushed to Coco and each grabbed one of her arms. They held her firmly while she thrashed.

Coco called out to Adrian for help. He turned slowly on his heel and stared at her with cold vacancy behind his eyes while the Queen began to shriek in terror.

Rudy was flung from his hiding spot in Coco's sleeve when the guards snatched her. He chose to fly a large loop around the chaos rather than fall to the ground.

The Queen was frozen in fear when she saw him. She sat and screamed, gaping at Rudy while he maneuvered through the people in the room.

She finally snapped out of her paralysis and screamed, "Smash it! Kill it!" The Queen flung her hand over her open mouth and pointed, following Rudy with her finger.

Not particularly wanting to be squashed, Rudy flew around the room looking for an escape. He found a door left slightly ajar that led to the courtyard.

The two guards held firmly to Coco. Adrian was

unresponsive under the spell of the spore. Rudy had abandoned Coco to save himself. She wanted to be mad at him for leaving her, but what could a fly really do to save her?

The Queen shot out of her seat and stomped over to Coco, each step an expression of her fury and hatred. "You dare to bring a fly to my Court?!" she shouted, so close to Coco that spit flew into her face.

"It's just a little fly. I don't see the problem. If you would have kept your goons off of me, you wouldn't have known he was there." Coco jerked an arm feebly.

"THAT ISN'T THE POINT!" the Queen shrieked. She threw her hands in the air and turned her back to Coco, stalking back and forth.

When the Queen's back was turned, the guard to Coco's right tightened his grip on her arm and hissed, "The Queen is terrified of flies. You've fucked up big, little sister."

The Queen turned to face Coco again with fire in her eye. The light bulb in place of her other eye was flashing erratically. She strode back over to Coco, and with each step her anger gave way to amusement. This confused and frightened Coco.

The Queen stood in front of her, smirking. Her lips parted slowly. She flashed her bear trap grin and locked eyes with Coco as she addressed the guards and waved a dismissive hand in the air. "Take her to the Chamber."

She turned, wrapped an arm through Adrian's, and marched away with him in tow. The Queen's skirts dragged in the dirt behind her while she stroked Adrian's arm and beamed up at him. He smiled back at her with mindless saccharine worship. Coco watched as the door shut behind them.

The guards dragged Coco through the courtyard and out a side door. They led her down a muddy, littered path. There were no other people around. Coco flailed wildly, trying to free herself from the grip of their calloused hands.

They arrived at a sturdy looking, squat structure with a large metal door where two guards stood. The two men holding Coco threw her at the guards' feet. She hit the ground face-first and tasted sickly, sour dirt.

"This one goes to the Chamber, by order of the Queen"

Coco looked up at the guards surrounding her.

The two at the door smirked down at her.

"On your feet." the fatter one said.

She obeyed. She was clearly outnumbered.

Pieces of wrought iron fencing in various shades of rust had all been welded together to form a heavy door. The guard inserted a large skeleton key into the lock and heaved his bulk against the door to force it open.

Inside was a jail. A dungeon. Aluminum siding and chain link all fused together with wrought iron reinforcement to keep a handful of prisoners trapped. Two oversized birdcages dangled from the ceiling where two men, one in each cage, squatted inside looking hungry and tired. They were covered in shit, as were their cages and the floor below them.

The guards shoved her through the dungeon, past the other prisoners to another large door on the other side of the room. The fat guard jammed a key in the lock and tried to turn it.

"This damn thing is jammed. Hang on to her." he fidgeted with his keys. He tried a different one.

While he busied himself with the task of keys, Coco couldn't help but wonder what was on the other side of that door. Her thoughts were rudely interrupted when she felt the hand of the thinner guard squeeze her ass.

Coco's elbow flew towards his face and struck a solid blow to his nose.

"Son of a bitch!" he screamed. He doubled over holding his face. Blood dripped from between his fingers.

The fat guard turned to see what had happened. He grabbed the wooden club from his holster and swung fiercely at Coco's head.

Coco's vision exploded with bright orange light and she crumpled into unconsciousness.

Seventeen

The stench woke Coco. She was afraid to open her eyes. She didn't want to know where she was, or the source of the smell.

The back of her head throbbed. She thought of the purple brain sucking spores and desperately groped under her mess of hair to check if one of them was on her. She walked her fingers nimbly over her scalp and found only a large lump from where the guard had hit her.

Coco avoided opening her eyes as long as she could. Soon the urge to vomit was so great she had no choice, if only to find somewhere to be sick. When she opened them, she had trouble focusing.

Her dress was pulled up around her waist. Through her gauzy eyes, the room appeared to be a padded cell. On the floor nearby was her silver g-string.

The room smelled like shit. Literally.

Without much time to analyze it, she could see there was nothing else in the room with her. Just four, off-white, quilted walls, with a floor and ceiling to match. Clearly the only place to vomit was in the corner.

Coco stood and pulled her dress down. The floor was soft and uneven. The heels of her shoes dug into the plastic quilted floor and tore holes in it. The more she walked, the more it tore, until the quilted cushions fell apart and brown paste oozed from the floor like old pus from a wound. The smell of shit was instantly stronger. Coco fell to her knees and retched violently into the corner.

Hot stomach acid and roasted cat meat sprayed onto the floor, mingling with the stuff already pooling under her from the brown seepage her heels had unleashed. It was all too much. Coco threw up until she was gagging on green foam and there was nothing left inside her stomach. She heaved until tears were streaming down her face. She just wanted to go home.

Coco sat up and wiped her face with her dress. She tore a layer of fabric from her skirt and tied it around her face. She looked around her cell.

The Chamber was a very small padded room, much like that of a mental institution. But this room was padded with used diapers. Judging from the slow fountains of shit squeezing through the holes her stilettos had torn, they weren't just baby diapers. Kernels of corn and peanuts were clearly visible in the brown muck. Coco dry heaved into her hands.

The door to the room was metal with a barred slat at eye level. Coco leapt up and pressed her face against it. She lifted her makeshift mask and gasped hungrily at the relatively fresh air on the other side with her face mashed against the bars. There didn't appear to be anyone guarding her. There also didn't appear to be a way out.

Coco stood with her face pressed to the bars until it hurt. She pressed her face so hard into the metal that she was sure it would bruise. But she didn't care. She would do anything to breathe something beside the fetid air of the Chamber. She watched the shadows in the dark hall outside the door, and waited for a guard to check on her.

Rudy flew through the bars and landed on the wall. "This place is fucking great!" He hopped about the room happier than Coco had ever seen him.

"It's not! It's terrible and I have to get out of here!"

Rudy laughed, "Sorry sweetheart. The guards throw you in, and then drag you out. When you're dead." He settled into one of the holes torn by Coco's shoes.

The fly sniffed the sludge, and rolled about giddily before he stopped and cocked his tiny bug head to one side. "You know, there is a way you could get out of here, but you aren't going to like it."

Coco wailed, "I'll do anything, I don't care! I have to get out of here!"

Rudy buzzed through the air and landed, with his petite shitty feet on Coco's nose. "Dig."

Eighteen

Coco hated that idea more than anything, but Rudy was right. There was no other way to get out of the Chamber, and the pointed heels of her shoes had already proven they could do damage to the floor. She tied another strip of fabric around her face, sat down and took off her shoes. She strapped them to her hands and began digging into the wall opposite the door.

Feces oozed out of each new wound she tore into the walls. It seeped into her shoes while she dug and squished between her fingers. The more the wall broke down, the more shit covered Coco's arms. When she stopped, she was up to her elbows in human waste. She shook her arms vigorously before she heaved her entire body against the wall. It only moved a few inches.

Barefoot, with shit oozing between her toes, Coco backed up to the door and got a good running start. She threw herself against the wall full-force. A large piece of it fell over, and Coco rode it to the ground. The rest of the wall fell around her.

She wriggled and dug her way out from the pile of shit-filled diapers and looked around. Coco was pretty sure she knew which direction the Castle was, so she started toward it. She was going to save Adrian, and make the Queen pay for what she had done.

Coco trekked on, covered in shit and baking in the sun. She didn't even care about the smell now that she had a true mission. She was going to save Adrian. She was going to save them all. Rudy had given up trying to talk to her. In her fury she stomped through the garbage muttering and swearing. Rudy took this opportunity to wallow around in the chunks of shit clinging to Coco's dress and arms.

"Coco...?"

A familiar voice called from the surrounding garbage.

Victor sat beneath an old camper shell, hiding from the blazing sun. He squinted at her in disbelief.

"Victor?"

He scurried from his hiding place like an excited cockroach and threw his arms around her.

She shoved him away. "What the fuck are you doing here?"

"You're alive!" he said. He looked at his streaked shirt, "And covered in shit." He grabbed her filthy, feces-coated hands. "Coco, I think I've gone completely mad. Arnie and I went for drinks after we... well, you know... and I crawled into that dumpster because I love you. I just needed to be near you." He pulled her close and nuzzled her matted hair. "And now I've found you! But this place is so strange. The flies talk to me. And the rats. And that old woman in the rotting meat house. I think I must have snapped."

Coco pulled away from Victor. She eyed him suspiciously. "You came to find me? But you threw me away. Like garbage."

"No! It was Arnie! I mean, I helped him. But you know how he gets. He's fucking terrifying. But I missed you. I crawled into the dumpster to be with you, and then I woke up here. There is something seriously fucking wrong with Waste Management Services."

"That's disgusting! You crawled into the dumpster to be with my dead body? You sick fuck!" She slapped him across the face with her shitty hand.

Victor stared at her, mouth hanging open and a shit-print pasted across his cheek. "But, but, I did it because I love you," he stammered.

Coco kneed him in the testicles.

Victor fell to his knees before he toppled onto his side into the fetal position and moaned.

Coco kicked him in the ribs and turned to walk away.

"Wait! You can't just leave me here!" he groaned.

She thought that she very well could. Victor was obviously sick. She wanted no part of his obscene lust for her. But it couldn't hurt to have a full-sized ally going into battle. Coco agreed to let him come along with her to the castle on the condition that he help her bring down the Queen once and for all.

Victor had also made an unlikely friend on his journey through the landfill—a rat named Theo.

Theo and the rest of the rats had been banished much like the flies. While the flies had been left to their own devices, the rats were placed on reservations outside the kingdom. Much like the flies, they were enraged at having been ousted from their homes.

"We're better off than the cats." Theo twitched his whiskers. "They're being held as a food supply. I guess that must be why the rats are still kept nearby, to feed the cats. Or in case they run out of cats."

Coco gagged, recalling the taste of cat meat, pre and post digestion.

They marched toward town, and devised their plan. Rudy went to gather their troops and fill them in on the plan. They would need all the flies. Coco hoped her plan would work. She hoped she could count on them.

Nineteen

The Queen was resting in her quarters—a converted horse trailer at the top of a stone tower. She was surrounded by knights with bulbous purple protrusions affixed to various areas of their bodies. Their legs, arms, faces and necks all pulsated with purple spores.

The affected knights fanned the Queen with newspapers, rubbed her calloused feet, and dusted her belongings. One of them swept the excess spores out the door and into a barrel where they were set on fire. Any knight without a task to perform stood over their Queen's bed staring at her with an expression of dumb adoration plastered across their face.

The Queen reclined on a battered velvet chaise lounge, with stuffing pouring from the seams and cigarette burns. She waved her hands and leisurely called out orders to the men filling her room.

The Queen was just beginning to drift off to sleep under the gentle breeze of the newspaper fan, when a servant burst into the room, startling her. "Your majesty! The girl has escaped!"

"She's what?!" the Queen launched herself off the chaise lounge onto her feet, "How? No one escapes the Chamber!"

"I went in to check on her and it seems she's dug her way out. I scouted the area, but she is nowhere to be found."

"Unacceptable!" the Queen shouted. She clapped loudly for the knights' attention. "Go and find her! Bring her to me!"

The knights marched out of her room, single file and spread out, scouring the kingdom for Coco.

"Dead or alive!" the Queen screamed from her window. "Bring me her fucking head on a plate! I'll eat her heart!"

Twenty

Coco needed to find a good place to corner the Queen once everything else was in place. She turned down a narrow alley, and there she saw Adrian. He was turning over boxes, looking inside holes in the wall. Looking for *her*.

"Adrian!" she called out and ran to him. He turned to her with that same cold expression. Only a faint glimmer of recognition flashed through his eyes as he approached her.

Coco threw her arms around him. Adrian stood perfectly still, a shell of who he once was. He did not smile. Coco was desperate to save him. He wrapped his hand tightly around her wrist and began to drag her from the alley, without a word.

"Where are we going?" Coco asked.

"To the Queen. She wants to eat your heart. My love will have the meal she desires." His words fell flat without any meaning behind them, like a drone.

Coco dug her feet into the ground and pulled away from his grip. "The hell she will! Adrian, please! Help me stop her."

"Stop her? The Queen will have whatever her heart desires. I want to make her happy. I love her," he said flatly.

"But you don't. She's brainwashed you. You wanted me! It's this spore. It's making you say these things. This isn't want you want." She pleaded with him, hoping to get through. Hoping that just maybe there was some small piece of him inside that remembered that he had cared for her almost instantly. That he liked her.

Adrian just stared at Coco with dead eyes and said, "You're covered in shit."

Coco looked around for something sharp. She found a large piece of broken glass on the ground and picked it up. Adrian grabbed her by the arm and pulled her toward the castle.

She played along, shuffling a few paces behind him. Once she was sure he was not going to turn around, she walked a bit closer. She held the glass deftly in her hand and slid it between the spore and Adrian's skin. She twisted the glass to pry the spore from his head. The spore made moist, slurping suction sounds as she peeled the thing off her knight's head.

Adrian stopped mid-stride. The spore landed on the ground with a squishy plop. It immediately began to squirm toward him, but before it could move an inch Coco impaled it with her glass shiv. She stabbed it once, twice, three times, until it was a puddle of purple goo.

Adrian bent over, one hand on a knee to support himself, the other clutching the back of his head. The area where the spore had been attached was a gory mess. The spore had eaten away a portion of Adrian's skull to get at his brain, and Coco could see the gray bloody tissue poking out from the wound. She knelt beside him as he slowly crumpled to the ground.

"Coco," he smiled at her through his apparent suffering. "I'm not going to make it. No one survives the spores." He coughed and rested his head in Coco's lap.

She looked down at him, knowing he was dying and there was nothing she could do about it. She cradled his head and stroked his hair. "But I didn't even get to know you. You CAN'T leave me. Please." Coco began to weep.

Adrian smiled weakly. His eyes slowly floated up and back, until they were stark white. Adrian let out a gurgling moan and he was gone.

Twenty-One

"There's been a slight change of plans," Coco said as she entered the shack beside the Gate. She dropped a rubber suit of armor in Victor's lap.

He sat in the dirt and fingered the tread looking up at her. He couldn't believe she was still alive. "Where's Adrian? And what's with all the blood on your dress?" Rudy buzzed around Coco, eagerly anticipating the culmination of their plan.

Coco looked down at the crimson stain that bloomed across the lap of her dress and said, "The blood and the suit are his. The spores can't be removed without killing the knights. Put that suit on, Victor. We're going to need you to pretend to be one of them to get me to the Queen. Let's get moving."

Victor put on Adrian's rubber suit, elated at the opportunity to be his love's knight in slimy armor. Once armored, he held Coco by the arms, and marched her through town.

The people in the kingdom turned and watched, but said nothing. Coco played at having been captured. The duo marched right into the castle, past the guards at the door and through many long corridors. Several knights raised an eyebrow of approval at Coco's capture, but made no other moves.

Victor soon realized that he had no idea where he was going. He had been dragging her in circles through the castle. They passed the same guard twice and on their third pass he stepped into their path.

"Lost?" he asked, eyeing Coco up and down.

"I've brought the Queen a present," Victor said. He

jerked Coco roughly by the arm. "Any idea where she is?"

The guard raised an eyebrow. "We all know she's in the Compost Garden, taking her mid-day nap."

"Must've slipped my mind. I've been out hunting for her. Not posted in a cozy hallway."

The guard's chest puffed out and he clenched his jaw. Victor said nothing, half expecting the knight to throw a punch.

Instead the guard said, "Look, I'm just doing my job. Take her to the Queen and get out of my face, alright?" He pointed down the hall behind him.

Victor shoved Coco down the corridor. They followed the sounds of soft snoring and grunting into the Compost Garden.

There were piles of various sized fruit, manure, and mulch, littered with egg shells and flower petals, arranged in the shape of a spiral.

Victor and Coco made their way through the maze, following the sound of the Queen snoring, which grew louder as they neared the center. They found her asleep in a hammock made of plastic six-pack rings hung between two pieces of rebar.

Coco strutted over to the hammock and pulled one side down to the ground. She let go and watched the Queen spill out.

The Queen floundered and sputtered, poking her head out from her mess of a dress. "You!" she shouted.

"Yes. Me." Coco stood over the Queen. She felt powerful wearing filth, the tattered dress, caked-on shit, and Adrian's blood. It was a new kind of power to her. Not like the power of sex—like she felt on stage, but REAL power.

The Queen tried to stand.

Coco planted a shit-splattered silver stiletto into her chest and kicked her back to the ground.

The Queen shouted for the guards.

Coco shouted for Rudy.

The Queen laughed "Your *fly*? He may give me the creeps, but he can't help you. My guards will STILL take you away!"

"Do you think they'll get here in time?" Coco smirked at the Queen, though she wasn't so sure herself. But if she'd learned anything from the years on stage, it was to fake it 'til you make it.

For the first time since her arrival, Coco saw fear flash across the Queen's face. They stared at each other in silence, waiting for the other to make the next move.

"What's that sound?" the Queen said, breaking their brief standoff.

The air around them was suddenly alive with vibration, and strangely shadier.

The Queen looked up at the sky, bewildered by the shadow that had abruptly fallen. Her mouth fell open in dismay and her shrill cries of terror were barely muffled by her hands, as she stood and ran from the center of the garden.

Rudy and thousands of his closest friends swarmed in a buzzing black cloud. They converged on the garden, following the Queen as she fled in panic through the spiral compost beds. She ran out of the garden and past the castle, too afraid to pay attention to where she was going.

Twenty-Two

Two knights rushed into the garden from the opposite side of the exiting queen. One of them had a purple blob attached to the side of his face, pulsating and transmitting false feelings of love and adoration to his brain.

This knight saw the black cloud of flies swooping in circles after the Queen and heard her cries of terror. He followed her. He ran as fast as he could—the undulation of the spore falling in time with the pumping of his arms. He hurtled compost heaps and threw himself over broken lawn gnomes and deck chairs decorating the path, desperate to catch up to the Queen he so adored.

The other knight shouted, "Hey! What the bloody fuck is going on out here?"

Victor turned to respond.

Before he could, the knight said, "Who are you? I've never seen you before. Get down! On your knees!"

Almost out of habit, Coco started to sink to the ground.

Victor remained on his feet but raised his hands. He stepped toward the guard. "I found this girl threatening our Queen. Glad you're here, man."

"I said, on the ground." The guard reached for his hip holster.

Victor continued to move toward him.

"Not another step," the guard ordered. He brandished a painted wooden cylinder and held it up to his mouth. "One more step and I'll do it."

"There's no need, man. We're on the same team." Victor flashed a weak smile at the guard.

"Victor, get *down*," Coco hissed.

"Victor, huh?" the guard scoffed. "Seems you're awfully familiar with the prisoner. How does she know your name? Why don't I? I've never seen you before."

"I'm new." Victor shrugged.

Victor's audacity caught the guard by surprise. He dropped his hands an inch or so from his face, ready to yell at the intruder. Victor rushed at him like a pro wrestler diving off of a turnbuckle—arms spread wide.

The guard raised the tube to his mouth, and blew a large burst of air into the mouthpiece.

A yellow, oblong item launched from the tube. As soon as it hit the air, it began to expand like a deformed bubble. It grew until it was the size and shape of a large squash. A thick, creamy fluid sloshed inside the jaundiced balloon.

Coco immediately identified the item as a condom. She knelt on the ground, motionless. She didn't run away so much because she was frozen with fear, more out of a sense of curiosity.

The condom soared through the air, landed with a squish on Victor's head, and snapped tight around his neck. The rubber contracted around his face, vacuum-sealing him inside. The lack of air caused the semen in the horrible balloon to bubble up around his face and into his nose.

Victor fell to the ground, groping at the condom trap and trying to tear through it. He desperately pulled at the tight seal around his neck. He flopped to the ground, kicking. Victor puked, and vomit puffed into the condom, sloshing around his face with the pearly white goo. He blew puffs of air out of his nose, trying to clear his nasal passages of old clotted semen and puke. He was suffocating. Victor clawed feebly at the ground and rolled onto his back. His arms went rigid. Muffled gurgles splattered the condom soup against the inflated rubber's walls. Victor's legs kicked wildly and then went still.

The guard smirked. He stood confidently before Coco, aiming his weird gun at her. Coco knelt in the damp filth, not moving. She had no desire to suffer the same fate as Victor.

Coco was well-versed in the silent language of men. So

she played along. She played helpless as he stood over her. She looked up at him feigning fear in her big, doe eyes. She started to ask, "What are you going to do with me?" but when she opened her mouth, the guard shoved his index finger in it. He slid it around and over her tongue, looking down at her, feeling superior and obviously aroused as he unsnapped his tire-tread codpiece, and pulled out his dick.

Coco looked up at him, pretending she didn't know what he wanted from her. He smiled down at her and stuck his little twitching cock into her mouth. She submitted for a few seconds—letting his small thing push between her lips. She didn't dare let him enjoy it too much, or get a grip on the back of her hair. Then she'd be stuck.

Coco watched as the guard moaned and let his head fall back. She waited until he was fully immersed in the moment. Then she bit down, hard, at the base of his dick. She could feel her bottom teeth touch the top set and she ground them together, working her jaw muscles back and forth.

He howled in agony and punched her in the side of the head. Coco let go, a mess of blood running down her chin.

The guard collapsed to the ground with his hands grasping his torn crotch. Blood squirted between his fingers. "Oh my God! Oh fucking God! You fucking cunt!" He shrieked and rolled wildly, grasping at the fountain of blood erupting between his legs.

Coco wiped her mouth with the back of her hand and stood up. "Not as good as you hoped?" She spat on him and kicked him in the face. Twice. Then once in the ribs for good measure, before she headed down the path the Queen had taken.

Once Coco was out of the Compost Garden, she needed only to look at the sky to find the Queen. Coco ran through the village toward the cloud. As she approached, she could hear the din of thousands of flies buzzing and the screams of the fleeing Queen.

Coco found the cloud dive-bombing the Queen, who was stuck in a gap in one of the village walls. A knight held the Queen's ankles. He had one foot against the wall for leverage while he tried to yank her free. She kicked her legs wildly, which made it difficult for the guard to hold onto them. The Queen hoarsely screamed, "Get me out of here!"

Her pleas degenerated into unintelligible sounds of horror. She sounded like she was choking. The Queen sputtered muffled cries and shrill wheezing. Her body convulsed. Her legs scissored out of the guard's grip, and shit exploded from under her tattered dress. Her legs stopped kicking. The Queen went still. The guard grabbed hold of her ankles again, and pulled back hard.

He spotted Coco in his peripheral vision as he tugged. "The Queen was trying to get away from the flies. She's terribly frightened of them. They cornered her here, and swarmed. She was screaming about fly shit and maggot eggs. She tried to cram herself through this hole."

Coco watched the pulsating orb attached to the guard's face fade from violet to gray. Then it withered and turned brown. The guard continued to talk and pull at the Queen's legs. Coco found it difficult to pay attention to his words.

The spore on his face turned black and began to crumble. The guard paused in his efforts and stared at the Queen's ankles in his hands. He dropped them, and took a step back, confused. He looked to Coco for an answer.

Coco reached out and quickly brushed the rest of the flaking black residue from his face.

Together, the guard and Coco managed to pull the Queen out from where she had lodged herself into the wall. They counted to three and each gave a good hard tug at her legs. The Queen popped out of the wall and landed face down, unmoving, as Coco and the guard fell to the ground in a heap. They exchanged looks and examined the prone monarch.

Coco nudged her with the toe of her shoe. She remained motionless. The guard wedged a rubber clad foot under her shoulder and rolled the Queen onto her side. Half of a rat hung from her mouth, bit in two by her sharp metal teeth. The Queen's one real eye was a meaty socket of pulpy eyeball oozing blood. Her face was frozen into a grotesque expression of agony.

The guard knelt and plucked the grisly remains of the rat from the dead Queen's mouth. He rolled her onto her back. Another rat popped its head out of her mangled eye-socket, pushing the masticated eyeball onto the Queen's cheek. Its whiskers were bloody and tiny bits of brain and eye-pulp clung to its snout. The rat twitched its whiskers and climbed from inside her head.

"Delicious," it said, licking its paws and scurrying away.

The guard asked Coco to help him drag the Queen's dead body back to the castle. "For ceremony," he pleaded when she initially refused.

Coco took pity on the bewildered guard and helped him. She felt plenty of closure, having avenged Adrian's death. She didn't need any ceremony. But she figured those poor spore-infested knights that were most likely trying to shake off the Queen's sex-spell all across her vile kingdom, and they would need something to find peace in their situation.

She grabbed an ankle.

Twenty-Three

They entered the courtyard dragging the Queen behind them—leaving a thick, sticky trail of blood. The guard stopped in the center of the courtyard and whistled loudly. Most of the knights had already stopped what they were doing when the pair had walked through the door. The remaining few turned with their mouths agape once they saw the Queen's mangled and rat-chewed face.

Coco looked around at the knights. All of the spores had dried up and died. All of the knights were free from the Queen's brainwashed version of love.

The courtyard fell silent as the guard climbed up on the dining table and raised his fist in the air. He pointed a bloody finger at Coco. "She killed the Queen!" he shouted.

Coco tensed, unsure of their response. The other knights looked from the shouting guard to Coco, and then around at each other.

Their silence gave way to a roar of applause and cheering. They rushed to Coco and kissed her shit-caked shoes and blood-coated hands and feet. She stood there for several moments in awe of the praise she was receiving.

"I don't follow," she said slowly.

The guard jumped down gleefully. He grabbed Coco by the hands and waltzed her through the crowd to the Queen's throne at the head of the table. "Sit!" he said, his voice dripping with joy.

Coco looked at the throne. It seemed comfortable enough—overstuffed, with burn marks and patches. And she was tired.

"You've saved us! We couldn't ask for a better, kinder

successor!" he said, brandishing the Queen's barbed wire and gemstone crown. He placed it in the nest of Coco's matted hair and for once she was glad that her hair was such a tangled mess. It was the only thing keeping the metal barbs from cutting into her scalp.

"Successor?" Coco asked. She reached up and touched the crown. She looked over the crowd of servants gathering. They all seemed overjoyed.

"You've killed the Queen! That makes you our *new* queen!" he shouted, both fists high in the air. "Long live the Queen!" the knight began to chant.

The crowd joined him. Soon the chant echoed from every mouth in the courtyard—knight, fly, rat, and whatever other weird creatures had heard the news.

When the uproarious chorus faded to laughter and murmuring, the guard turned to Coco, "As Queen, what will be your first act?"

Coco surveyed the crowd, unsure of what one was supposed to do when ruling a kingdom of trash. Her eyes fell upon the knight who had groped her in the jail. His arms were crossed over his chest. He glared at Coco with one black eye and some crusted blood around his nose.

Coco laughed and pointed to him. "Off with his head!"

Constance Ann Fitzgerald lives in the Bay Area where she works in an adult shop, collecting stories about creeps. She can often be found talking to dogs and scribbling in notebooks. This is her first novella.

BIZARRO BOOKS

CATALOG   FALL 2011

ERASERHEAD PRESS

Your major resource for the bizarro fiction genre:

WWW.BIZARROCENTRAL.COM

Introduce yourselves to the bizarro fiction genre and all of its authors with the Bizarro Starter Kit series. Each volume features short novels and short stories by ten of the leading bizarro authors, designed to give you a perfect sampling of the genre for only $10.

BB-0X1
"The Bizarro Starter Kit" (Orange)

Featuring D. Harlan Wilson, Carlton Mellick III, Jeremy Robert Johnson, Kevin L Donihe, Gina Ranalli, Andre Duza, Vincent W. Sakowski, Steve Beard, John Edward Lawson, and Bruce Taylor. **236 pages $10**

BB-0X2
"The Bizarro Starter Kit" (Blue)

Featuring Ray Fracalossy, Jeremy C. Shipp, Jordan Krall, Mykle Hansen, Andersen Prunty, Eckhard Gerdes, Bradley Sands, Steve Aylett, Christian TeBordo, and Tony Rauch. **244 pages $10**

BB-0X2
"The Bizarro Starter Kit" (Purple)

Featuring Russell Edson, Athena Villaverde, David Agranoff, Matthew Revert, Andrew Goldfarb, Jeff Burk, Garrett Cook, Kris Saknussemm, Cody Goodfellow, and Cameron Pierce **264 pages $10**

BB-001 **"The Kafka Effekt" D. Harlan Wilson** — A collection of forty-four irreal short stories loosely written in the vein of Franz Kafka, with more than a pinch of William S. Burroughs sprinkled on top. **211 pages $14**

BB-002 **"Satan Burger" Carlton Mellick III** — The cult novel that put Carlton Mellick III on the map ... Six punks get jobs at a fast food restaurant owned by the devil in a city violently overpopulated by surreal alien cultures. **236 pages $14**

BB-003 **"Some Things Are Better Left Unplugged" Vincent Sakwoski** — Join The Man and his Nemesis, the obese tabby, for a nightmare roller coaster ride into this postmodern fantasy. **152 pages $10**

BB-004 **"Shall We Gather At the Garden?" Kevin L Donihe** — Donihe's Debut novel. Midgets take over the world, The Church of Lionel Richie vs. The Church of the Byrds, plant porn and more! **244 pages $14**

BB-005 **"Razor Wire Pubic Hair" Carlton Mellick III** — A genderless humandildo is purchased by a razor dominatrix and brought into her nightmarish world of bizarre sex and mutilation. **176 pages $11**

BB-006 **"Stranger on the Loose" D. Harlan Wilson** — The fiction of Wilson's 2nd collection is planted in the soil of normalcy, but what grows out of that soil is a dark, witty, otherworldly jungle... **228 pages $14**

BB-007 **"The Baby Jesus Butt Plug" Carlton Mellick III** — Using clones of the Baby Jesus for anal sex will be the hip sex fetish of the future. **92 pages $10**

BB-008 **"Fishyfleshed" Carlton Mellick III** — The world of the past is an illogical flatland lacking in dimension and color, a sick-scape of crispy squid people wandering the desert for no apparent reason. **260 pages $14**

BB-009 **"Dead Bitch Army" Andre Duza** — Step into a world filled with racist teenagers, cannibals, 100 warped Uncle Sams, automobiles with razor-sharp teeth, living graffiti, and a pissed-off zombie bitch out for revenge. **344 pages $16**

BB-010 **"The Menstruating Mall" Carlton Mellick III** — "The Breakfast Club meets Chopping Mall as directed by David Lynch." - Brian Keene **212 pages $12**

BB-011 **"Angel Dust Apocalypse" Jeremy Robert Johnson** — Meth-heads, man-made monsters, and murderous Neo-Nazis. "Seriously amazing short stories..." - Chuck Palahniuk, author of Fight Club **184 pages $11**

BB-012 **"Ocean of Lard" Kevin L Donihe / Carlton Mellick III** — A parody of those old Choose Your Own Adventure kid's books about some very odd pirates sailing on a sea made of animal fat. **176 pages $12**

BB-015 **"Foop!" Chris Genoa** — Strange happenings are going on at Dactyl, Inc, the world's first and only time travel tourism company.
"A surreal pie in the face!" - Christopher Moore **300 pages $14**

BB-020 **"Punk Land" Carlton Mellick III** — In the punk version of Heaven, the anarchist utopia is threatened by corporate fascism and only Goblin, Mortician's sperm, and a blue-mohawked female assassin named Shark Girl can stop them. **284 pages $15**

BB-027 **"Siren Promised" Jeremy Robert Johnson & Alan M Clark** — Nominated for the Bram Stoker Award. A potent mix of bad drugs, bad dreams, brutal bad guys, and surreal/incredible art by Alan M. Clark. **190 pages $13**

BB-031**"Sea of the Patchwork Cats" Carlton Mellick III** — A quiet dreamlike tale set in the ashes of the human race. For Mellick enthusiasts who also adore The Twilight Zone. **112 pages $10**

BB-032 **"Extinction Journals" Jeremy Robert Johnson** — An uncanny voyage across a newly nuclear America where one man must confront the problems associated with loneliness, insane dieties, radiation, love, and an ever-evolving cockroach suit with a mind of its own. **104 pages $10**

BB-037 **"The Haunted Vagina" Carlton Mellick III** — It's difficult to love a woman whose vagina is a gateway to the world of the dead. **132 pages $10**

BB-043 **"War Slut" Carlton Mellick III** — Part "1984," part "Waiting for Godot," and part action horror video game adaptation of John Carpenter's "The Thing." **116 pages $10**

BB-047 **"Sausagey Santa" Carlton Mellick III** — A bizarro Christmas tale featuring Santa as a piratey mutant with a body made of sausages. 124 pages $10

BB-048 **"Misadventures in a Thumbnail Universe" Vincent Sakowski** — Dive deep into the surreal and satirical realms of neo-classical Blender Fiction, filled with television shoes and flesh-filled skies. **120 pages $10**

BB-053 **"Ballad of a Slow Poisoner" Andrew Goldfarb** — Millford Mutterwurst sat down on a Tuesday to take his afternoon tea, and made the unpleasant discovery that his elbows were becoming flatter. **128 pages $10**

BB-055 **"Help! A Bear is Eating Me" Mykle Hansen** — The bizarro, heartwarming, magical tale of poor planning, hubris and severe blood loss...
150 pages $11

BB-056 **"Piecemeal June" Jordan Krall** — A man falls in love with a living sex doll, but with love comes danger when her creator comes after her with crab-squid assassins. **90 pages $9**

BB-058 **"The Overwhelming Urge" Andersen Prunty** — A collection of bizarro tales by Andersen Prunty. **150 pages $11**

BB-059 **"Adolf in Wonderland" Carlton Mellick III** — A dreamlike adventure that takes a young descendant of Adolf Hitler's design and sends him down the rabbit hole into a world of imperfection and disorder. **180 pages $11**

BB-061 **"Ultra Fuckers" Carlton Mellick III** — Absurdist suburban horror about a couple who enter an upper middle class gated community but can't find their way out. **108 pages $9**

BB-062 **"House of Houses" Kevin L. Donihe** — An odd man wants to marry his house. Unfortunately, all of the houses in the world collapse at the same time in the Great House Holocaust. Now he must travel to House Heaven to find his departed fiancee. **172 pages $11**

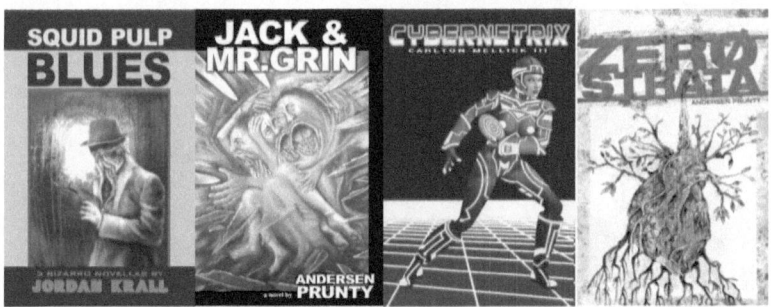

BB-064 **"Squid Pulp Blues" Jordan Krall** — In these three bizarro-noir novellas, the reader is thrown into a world of murderers, drugs made from squid parts, deformed gun-toting veterans, and a mischievous apocalyptic donkey. **204 pages $12**

BB-065 **"Jack and Mr. Grin" Andersen Prunty** — "When Mr. Grin calls you can hear a smile in his voice. Not a warm and friendly smile, but the kind that seizes your spine in fear. You don't need to pay your phone bill to hear it. That smile is in every line of Prunty's prose." - Tom Bradley. **208 pages $12**

BB-066 **"Cybernetrix" Carlton Mellick III** — What would you do if your normal everyday world was slowly mutating into the video game world from Tron? **212 pages $12**

BB-072 **"Zerostrata" Andersen Prunty** — Hansel Nothing lives in a tree house, suffers from memory loss, has a very eccentric family, and falls in love with a woman who runs naked through the woods every night. **144 pages $11**

BB-073 "The Egg Man" Carlton Mellick III — It is a world where humans reproduce like insects. Children are the property of corporations, and having an enormous ten-foot brain implanted into your skull is a grotesque sexual fetish. Mellick's industrial urban dystopia is one of his darkest and grittiest to date. **184 pages $11**

BB-074 "Shark Hunting in Paradise Garden" Cameron Pierce — A group of strange humanoid religious fanatics travel back in time to the Garden of Eden to discover it is invested with hundreds of giant flying maneating sharks. **150 pages $10**

BB-075 "Apeshit" Carlton Mellick III - Friday the 13th meets Visitor Q. Six hipster teens go to a cabin in the woods inhabited by a deformed killer. An incredibly fucked-up parody of B-horror movies with a bizarro slant. **192 pages $12**

BB-076 "Fuckers of Everything on the Crazy Shitting Planet of the Vomit At smosphere" Mykle Hansen - Three bizarro satires. Monster Cocks, Journey to the Center of Agnes Cuddlebottom, and Crazy Shitting Planet. **228 pages $12**

BB-077 "The Kissing Bug" Daniel Scott Buck — In the tradition of Roald Dahl, Tim Burton, and Edward Gorey, comes this bizarro anti-war children's story about a bohemian conenose kissing bug who falls in love with a human woman. **116 pages $10**

BB-078 "MachoPoni" Lotus Rose — It's My Little Pony... *Bizarro* style! A long time ago Poniworld was split in two. On one side of the Jagged Line is the Pastel Kingdom, a magical land of music, parties, and positivity. On the other side of the Jagged Line is Dark Kingdom inhabited by an army of undead ponies. **148 pages $11**

BB-079 "The Faggiest Vampire" Carlton Mellick III — A Roald Dahl-esque children's story about two faggy vampires who partake in a mustache competition to find out which one is truly the faggiest. **104 pages $10**

BB-080 "Sky Tongues" Gina Ranalli — The autobiography of Sky Tongues, the biracial hermaphrodite actress with tongues for fingers. Follow her strange life story as she rises from freak to fame. **204 pages $12**

BB-081 **"Washer Mouth" Kevin L. Donihe** - A washing machine becomes human and pursues his dream of meeting his favorite soap opera star. **244 pages $11**

BB-082 **"Shatnerquake" Jeff Burk** - All of the characters ever played by William Shatner are suddenly sucked into our world. Their mission: hunt down and destroy the real William Shatner. **100 pages $10**

BB-083 **"The Cannibals of Candyland" Carlton Mellick III** - There exists a race of cannibals that are made of candy. They live in an underground world made out of candy. One man has dedicated his life to killing them all. **170 pages $11**

BB-084 **"Slub Glub in the Weird World of the Weeping Willows"** **Andrew Goldfarb** - The charming tale of a blue glob named Slub Glub who helps the weeping willows whose tears are flooding the earth. There are also hyenas, ghosts, and a voodoo priest **100 pages $10**

BB-085 **"Super Fetus" Adam Pepper** - Try to abort this fetus and he'll kick your ass! **104 pages $10**

BB-086 **"Fistful of Feet" Jordan Krall** - A bizarro tribute to spaghetti westerns, featuring Cthulhu-worshipping Indians, a woman with four feet, a crazed gunman who is obsessed with sucking on candy, Syphilis-ridden mutants, sexually transmitted tattoos, and a house devoted to the freakiest fetishes. **228 pages $12**

BB-087 **"Ass Goblins of Auschwitz" Cameron Pierce** - It's Monty Python meets Nazi exploitation in a surreal nightmare as can only be imagined by Bizarro author Cameron Pierce. **104 pages $10**

BB-088 **"Silent Weapons for Quiet Wars" Cody Goodfellow** - "This is high-end psychological surrealist horror meets bottom-feeding low-life crime in a techno-thrilling science fiction world full of Lovecraft and magic..." -John Skipp **212 pages $12**

BB-089 **"Warrior Wolf Women of the Wasteland" Carlton Mellick III**
— Road Warrior Werewolves versus McDonaldland Mutants...post-apocalyptic fiction has never been quite like this. **316 pages $13**

BB-091 **"Super Giant Monster Time" Jeff Burk** — A tribute to choose your own adventures and Godzilla movies. Will you escape the giant monsters that are rampaging the fuck out of your city and shit? Or will you join the mob of alien-controlled punk rockers causing chaos in the streets? What happens next depends on you. **188 pages $12**

BB-092 **"Perfect Union" Cody Goodfellow** — "Cronenberg's THE FLY on a grand scale: human/insect gene-spliced body horror, where the human hive politics are as shocking as the gore." -John Skipp. **272 pages $13**

BB-093 **"Sunset with a Beard" Carlton Mellick III** — 14 stories of surreal science fiction. **200 pages $12**

BB-094 **"My Fake War" Andersen Prunty** — The absurd tale of an unlikely soldier forced to fight a war that, quite possibly, does not exist. It's Rambo meets Waiting for Godot in this subversive satire of American values and the scope of the human imagination. **128 pages $11**

BB-095 **"Lost in Cat Brain Land" Cameron Pierce** — Sad stories from a surreal world. A fascist mustache, the ghost of Franz Kafka, a desert inside a dead cat. Primordial entities mourn the death of their child. The desperate serve tea to mysterious creatures. A hopeless romantic falls in love with a pterodactyl. And much more. **152 pages $11**

BB-096 **"The Kobold Wizard's Dildo of Enlightenment +2" Carlton Mellick III** — A Dungeons and Dragons parody about a group of people who learn they are only made up characters in an AD&D campaign and must find a way to resist their nerdy teenaged players and retarded dungeon master in order to survive. 232 **pages $12**

BB-098 **"A Hundred Horrible Sorrows of Ogner Stump" Andrew Goldfarb** — Goldfarb's acclaimed comic series. A magical and weird journey into the horrors of everyday life. **164 pages $11**

BB-099 **"Pickled Apocalypse of Pancake Island" Cameron Pierce**—A demented fairy tale about a pickle, a pancake, and the apocalypse. **102 pages $8**

BB-100 **"Slag Attack" Andersen Prunty**— Slag Attack features four visceral, noir stories about the living, crawling apocalypse.A slag is what survivors are calling the slug-like maggots raining from the sky, burrowing inside people, and hollowing out their flesh and their sanity. **148 pages $11**

BB-101 **"Slaughterhouse High" Robert Devereaux**—A place where schools are built with secret passageways, rebellious teens get zippers installed in their mouths and genitals, and once a year, on that special night, one couple is slaughtered and the bits of their bodies are kept as souvenirs. **304 pages $13**

BB-102 **"The Emerald Burrito of Oz" John Skipp & Marc Levinthal** —OZ IS REAL! Magic is real! The gate is really in Kansas! And America is finally allowing Earth tourists to visit this weird-ass, mysterious land. But when Gene of Los Angeles heads off for summer vacation in the Emerald City, little does he know that a war is brewing...a war that could destroy both worlds. **280 pages $13**

BB-103 **"The Vegan Revolution... with Zombies" David Agranoff**— When there's no more meat in hell, the vegans will walk the earth. **160 pages $11**

BB-104 **"The Flappy Parts" Kevin L Donihe**—Poems about bunnies, LSD, and police abuse. You know, things that matter. 132 **pages $11**

BB-105 **"Sorry I Ruined Your Orgy" Bradley Sands**—Bizarro humorist Bradley Sands returns with one of the strangest, most hilarious collections of the year. **130 pages $11**

BB-106 **"Mr. Magic Realism" Bruce Taylor**—Like Golden Age science fiction comics written by Freud, *Mr. Magic Realism* is a strange, insightful adventure that spans the furthest reaches of the galaxy, exploring the hidden caverns in the hearts and minds of men, women, aliens, and biomechanical cats. **152 pages $11**

BB-107 **"Zombies and Shit" Carlton Mellick III**—"Battle Royale" meets "Return of the Living Dead." Mellick's bizarro tribute to the zombie genre. **308 pages $13**

BB-108 **"The Cannibal's Guide to Ethical Living" Mykle Hansen**— Over a five star French meal of fine wine, organic vegetables and human flesh, a lunatic delivers a witty, chilling, disturbingly sane argument in favor of eating the rich.. **184 pages $11**

BB-109 **"Starfish Girl" Athena Villaverde**—In a post-apocalyptic underwater dome society, a girl with a starfish growing from her head and an assassin with sea anenome hair are on the run from a gang of mutant fish men. **160 pages $11**

BB-110 **"Lick Your Neighbor" Chris Genoa**—Mutant ninjas, a talking whale, kung fu masters, maniacal pilgrims, and an alcoholic clown populate Chris Genoa's surreal, darkly comical and unnerving reimagining of the first Thanksgiving. **303 pages $13**

BB-111 **"Night of the Assholes" Kevin L. Donihe**—A plague of assholes is infecting the countryside. Normal everyday people are transforming into jerks, snobs, dicks, and douchebags. And they all have only one purpose: to make your life a living hell.. **192 pages $11**

BB-112 **"Jimmy Plush, Teddy Bear Detective" Garrett Cook**—Hardboiled cases of a private detective trapped within a teddy bear body. **180 pages $11**

BB-113 **"The Deadheart Shelters" Forrest Armstrong**—The hip hop lovechild of William Burroughs and Dali... **144 pages $11**

BB-114 **"Eyeballs Growing All Over Me... Again" Tony Raugh**— Absurd, surreal, playful, dream-like, whimsical, and a lot of fun to read. **144 pages $11**

BB-115 **"Whargoul" Dave Brockie** — From the killing grounds of Stalingrad to the death camps of the holocaust. From torture chambers in Iraq to race riots in the United States, the Whargoul was there, killing and raping. **244 pages $12**

BB-116 **"By the Time We Leave Here, We'll Be Friends" J. David Osborne** — A David Lynchian nightmare set in a Russian gulag, where its prisoners, guards, traitors, soldiers, lovers, and demons fight for survival and their own rapidly deteriorating humanity. **168 pages $11**

BB-117 **"Christmas on Crack" edited by Carlton Mellick III** — Perverted Christmas Tales for the whole family! . . . as long as every member of your family is over the age of 18. **168 pages $11**

BB-118 **"Crab Town" Carlton Mellick III** — Radiation fetishists, balloon people, mutant crabs, sail-bike road warriors, and a love affair between a woman and an H-Bomb. This is one mean asshole of a city. Welcome to Crab Town. **100 pages $8**

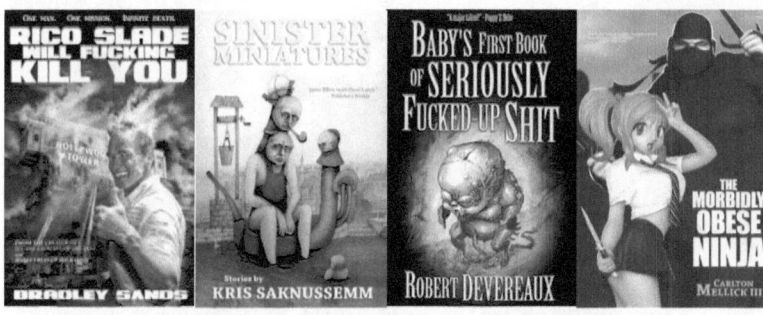

BB-119 **"Rico Slade Will Fucking Kill You" Bradley Sands** — Rico Slade is an action hero. Rico Slade can rip out a throat with his bare hands. Rico Slade's favorite food is the honey-roasted peanut. Rico Slade will fucking kill everyone. A novel. **122 pages $8**

BB-120 **"Sinister Miniatures" Kris Saknussemm** — The definitive collection of short fiction by Kris Saknussemm, confirming that he is one of the best, most daring writers of the weird to emerge in the twenty-first century. **180 pages $11**

BB-121 **"Baby's First Book of Seriously Fucked up Shit" Robert Devereaux** — Ten stories of the strange, the gross, and the just plain fucked up from one of the most original voices in horror. **176 pages $11**

BB-122 **"The Morbidly Obese Ninja" Carlton Mellick III** — These days, if you want to run a successful company . . . you're going to need a lot of ninjas. **92 pages $8**

BB-123 **"Abortion Arcade" Cameron Pierce** — An intoxicating blend of body horror and midnight movie madness, reminiscent of early David Lynch and the splatterpunks at their most sublime. **172 pages $11**

BB-124 **"Black Hole Blues" Patrick Wensink** — A hilarious double helix of country music and physics. **196 pages $11**

BB-125 **"Barbarian Beast Bitches of the Badlands" Carlton Mellick III** — Three prequels and sequels to *Warrior Wolf Women of the Wasteland.* **284 pages $13**

BB-126 **"The Traveling Dildo Salesman" Kevin L. Donihe** — A nightmare comedy about destiny, faith, and sex toys. Also featuring Donihe's most lurid and infamous short stories: *Milky Agitation, Two-Way Santa, The Helen Mower, Living Room Zombies,* and *Revenge of the Living Masturbation Rag.* **108 pages $8**

BB-127 **"Metamorphosis Blues" Bruce Taylor** — Enter a land of love beasts, intergalactic cowboys, and rock 'n roll. A land where Sears Catalogs are doorways to insanity and men keep mysterious black boxes. Welcome to the monstrous mind of Mr. Magic Realism. **136 pages $11**

BB-128 **"The Driver's Guide to Hitting Pedestrians" Andersen Prunty** — A pocket guide to the twenty-three most painful things in life, written by the most well-adjusted man in the universe. **108 pages $8**

BB-129 **"Island of the Super People" Kevin Shamel** — Four students and their anthropology professor journey to a remote island to study its indigenous population. But this is no ordinary native culture. They're super heroes and villains with flesh costumes and out-landish abilities like self-detonation, musical eyelashes, and microwave hands. **194 pages $11**

BB-130 **"Fantastic Orgy" Carlton Mellick III** — Shark Sex, mutant cats, and strange sexually transmitted diseases. Featuring the stories: *Candy-coated, Ear Cat, Fantastic Orgy, City Hobgoblins,* and *Porno in August.* **136 pages $9**

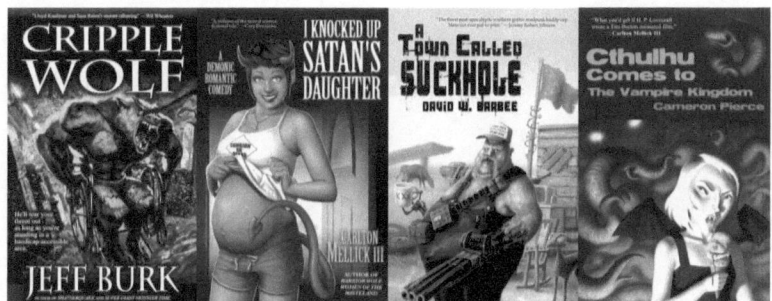

BB-131 **"Cripple Wolf" Jeff Burk** — Part man. Part wolf. 100% crippled. Also including *Punk Rock Nursing Home, Adrift with Space Badgers, Cook for Your Life, Just Another Day in the Park, Frosty and the Full Monty,* and *House of Cats.* **152 pages $10**

BB-132 **"I Knocked Up Satan's Daughter" Carlton Mellick III** — An adorable, violent, fantastical love story. A romantic comedy for the bizarro fiction reader. **152 pages $10**

BB-133 **"A Town Called Suckhole" David W. Barbee** — Far into the future, in the nuclear bowels of post-apocalyptic Dixie, there is a town. A town of derelict mobile homes, ancient junk, and mutant wildlife. A town of slack jawed rednecks who bask in the splendors of moonshine and mud boggin'. A town dedicated to the bloody and demented legacy of the Old South. A town called Suckhole. **144 pages $10**

BB-134 **"Cthulhu Comes to the Vampire Kingdom" Cameron Pierce** — What you'd get if H. P. Lovecraft wrote a Tim Burton animated film. **148 pages $11**

BB-135 **"I am Genghis Cum" Violet LeVoit** — From the savage Arctic tundra to post-partum mutations to your missing daughter's unmarked grave, join visionary madwoman Violet LeVoit in this non-stop eight-story onslaught of full-tilt Bizarro punk lit thrills. **124 pages $9**

BB-136 **"Haunt" Laura Lee Bahr** — A tripping-balls Los Angeles noir, where a mysterious dame drags you through a time-warping Bizarro hall of mirrors. **316 pages $13**

BB-137 **"Amazing Stories of the Flying Spaghetti Monster" edited by Cameron Pierce** — Like an all-spaghetti evening of Adult Swim, the Flying Spaghetti Monster will show you the many realms of His Noodly Appendage. Learn of those who worship him and the lives he touches in distant, mysterious ways. **228 pages $12**

BB-138 **"Wave of Mutilation" Douglas Lain** — A dream-pop exploration of modern architecture and the American identity, *Wave of Mutilation* is a Zen finger trap for the 21st century. **100 pages $8**